SEXUAL DIVERSITY AND PERVERSITY IN CALIFORNIA

First Edition

Published by The Nazca Plains Corporation
Las Vegas, Nevada
2008

ISBN: 978-1-934625-64-4

Published by

The Nazca Plains Corporation ®
4640 Paradise Rd, Suite 141
Las Vegas NV 89109-8000

PUBLISHER'S NOTE
SEXUAL DIVERSITY AND PERVERSITY IN CALIFORNIA is a work of fiction created wholly by *Tim Desmondes'* imagination. All characters are fictional and any resemblance to any persons living or deceased is purely by accident. No portion of this book reflects any real person or events.

Cover, David Liu and Lev Dolgatshjov
Art Director, Blake Stephens

DEDICATION

To that diverse, multi-ethnic, multi-sexual, fascinating group of people who call themselves Californians. No book could possibly do justice to you. But, I lift my wine glass to you nonetheless.

SEXUAL DIVERSITY AND PERVERSITY IN CALIFORNIA

First Edition

Tim Desmondes

TABLE OF CONTENTS

INTRODUCTION

I was born and raised in Los Angeles. And as an adult I have dwelt in many parts of California.

I have been a resident of her cities, suburbs, and villages. I have lived in her deserts, her valleys, and her beach towns.

All my life I have encountered the diversity, and, yes, the perversity of the people of my native state.

In my previous book, *Sex and Loathing in Hollywood,* I explored the way of life of the denizens of a microcosm of the entire state of California.

Within the following pages I have extended my vision to the macrocosm.

However, even here, I could not leave out another Hollywood story.

Tim Desmondes

PART ONE

THE TRANSGENDER HOTEL

CHAPTER ONE
AS TOLD BY TILLY BLAINE

If you read the credits when you go to the movies, you've seen my name. Costume designer – Tilly Blaine. I've been one of the chief costumers at Olympic Studios for several years now. So I've had my hands on most of the actors and actresses at Olympic, including the extras. I know when to cop a feel and when not to. When we costumers let our hands slip onto juicy property, we consider that part of our "psychic income."

Since I swing in the direction of Sappho, when I'm working with a starlet who needs a bustier designed for a cameo, I have been known to salivate as I run my hands over a particularly tasty pair of knockers.

I've bedded more than my share of quim. Another ancillary benefit of my trade. But no matter how many dolls I had pleasured, I was still frustrated. I'd never been able to make it with my best friend, Olivia Axelrod.

Olivia and I had been good friends, then best friends, since we were fifteen. We were in the same class at Hollywood High. She lived on Sycamore and I lived on Willoughby, so we were only about a ten minute walk away from each other's home.

I'd wanted to get into her pants even back then. We had sleepovers at her place and at mine. And we kissed each other a lot. We pretended that was practice for when boys would be making out with us. I always tried to cop a feel either upstairs or down. But she always fended me off. She claimed that was to keep her in practice so she could keep the boys from getting too fresh.

So, although we were friends, and even best friends, I was never able to get it on with her. I had great old times with Gloria, Sophie, Jeanette, and other girls. But not with Olivia.

When we were juniors in high school, Olivia started going steady with Mike. She let him do everything to her that I wanted to do. And of course, more. And, if you must know, I was jealous of him.

I knew something special about Mike. I saw how he was with the other guys. He was as queer for dudes as I was for chicks. When you're a citizen of Queer Nation you know those things. I tried to convince Olivia that her boyfriend liked boys. She just laughed me off.

Mike went to college at the Hollywood School of Design. I went there too, and maintained a good friendship with him. It was a way of assuring contact with Olivia

Mike and Olivia got married. I was maid of honor at the wedding. And on their wedding night my friend Gloria and I had a night of Cosmopolitans and sex. Gloria had a violent crush on Olivia (and still does, for that matter). So we took turns laying an ersatz Mike and bedding a make-believe Olivia. We got kind of hysterical as we improvised with the strap-on.

Mike and I both landed jobs at Olympic. He's one of the set designers. And, I've got to admit, a damned good one. He did all the sets for that tetralogy of Rob Roberts. No Academy Awards, or even a nomination. But his work is good. I did the costumes for those four pix, so Mike and I were in contact a lot. Which made it easy for me to keep close contact with his wife, who continued to be my obsession.

Don't get the idea I don't like Mike. I do. I'm jealous as Hell of him. He's in bed with my darling most nights. But I know he was fucking several of the guys at the studio, too. I could tell he had something pretty special with Karl Tepes in particular. You've seen Karl. Character actor. Plays mainly gangsters and tough guys. Did you happen to see *Vampires at the O.K. Corral?* Behind all that makeup, Karl's the one who played Radu, Dracula's cowboy brother.

I never stopped putting the moves on Olivia. She put me off with her laughs and giggles. It didn't stop us from being good friends. But my frustration was as strong then as it had been back in high school.

Back when they were filming *Showdown in Loredo* I thought I saw my chance. It was Saturday and I was at Mike and Olivia's place up on Franklin. Olivia and I were downing wine coolers while Mike was flitting back and forth from his workroom into the sun parlor where the wine was meeting the schnapps.

Olivia was wearing a tank top that showed off her lovely tits to their best advantage. I could have dived down into that cleavage and died. And the short shorts she had on rode across her mound in such a way as to make my twat clench.

"You know, Olivia," I said. "When I see you in that outfit I fairly drench my panties."

She laughed that off, like she always did. She knew the effect she had on me. She'd always thought it was kind of a joke.

"Oh, Tilly," she giggled. "What you need is a good man."

"I tried a man once," I told her. "That's all it took to convince me I'm only horny for girls. I've tried to convince you to try it. It beats sex with male pigs all to shit. You've admitted you'd like to try it."

We'd had this discussion a million times. Back in high school she really seemed to only go for guys. But after she got married and settled down with Mike she began to think she just might be missing something. I'd tell her of my romps with the girls, and it kind of turned her on. But she insisted she would never cheat on Mike.

"What if you found out he was cheating on you?" I'd ask. I didn't ask that question once. I'd asked it hundreds of times. And her answer was always more or less the same.

"If I ever found he wandered, I'd be tempted."

I would then ask if she would go to Eleutheria with me if she knew Mike was "wandering." And her answer was always just to nod a shy "yes."

If you're not part of the Hollywood crowd you probably don't know much about Villa Eleutheria. It's up in the Hollywood Hills near Ridgerton Drive. I wouldn't want to tell you exactly what street it's on. The location is divulged only by word of mouth from a patron to someone who is known to be cool. It just looks like a large comfortable house overlooking Hollywood below. It's built on a ledge with a cantilevered deck that can't be viewed from the road. But I've already said too much about its location.

What it is is a sexual refuge. It's set up for any sexual taste. Anything goes at Eleutheria: S/M, bondage, trans-gender, cross-dressing…name it. You just let Madame Alexander know the set-up you want and…voilà!

I'd told Olivia about Eleutheria scores of times. And I knew she was really intrigued.

Mike was a friend, a buddy. But I had to "out" him if I was to get Olivia to Eleutheria and get into her pants. I would do it in a minute.

I was sitting there soaking in Olivia's charms while feeling tingles run from my boobs to my pussy and fantasizing about what I would do with that body if I could ever get her to agree to ride up into the hills with me to my favorite sexual refuge. My hands and tongue itched for a feel of that yummy flesh. I'd give just about anything to press my naked body against the nudity behind that outfit she was wearing. It made me wild just thinking about how it would be to get my face down there into her koozie and smell it, lick it, love it. I told her she was making me horny. And what I'd like to do to her scrumptious body.

Like she always did when I got into my recurrent theme about how she turned me on, she changed the subject to business.

"That film you and Mike are working on sounds like it should be a big success."

"Showdown in Loredo?" I replied. "It should do well. It's part two of Rob Roberts' tetralogy staring Tex McCall and Crusher Carney. The public eats up everything Rob writes and produces. I love doing the Western costumes for this one. Particularly the dancing girls and whores in the saloon scenes. And Mike's sketches for the sets are really quite good. Your husband Mike excels at what he does."

"Yes," Olivia answered. "I'm proud of Mike and his work. This weekend he's going to fly down to Loredo with Rob Roberts to take some photos. He wants the sets to look authentic."

Wait a minute here. Just a God damned minute. In Rob's workroom at the studio the walls were covered with photographs of Loredo. Rob had gone to Loredo and stayed a month there taking pictures and doing local research for the picture. We were up to our asses in photographs of Loredo. I could tell there was something really fishy going on. I could smell that Mike was going away on a weekend date. Probably with Karl Tepes.

There was no reason to express my doubts to Olivia yet. All in good time.

"How do you know Mike's going to Loredo?" I asked.

"Because he told me so."

"He told you he's going with Rob? This weekend? To Loredo?"

"Yes," she said patiently, as though speaking to a child. "He told me he's going with Rob. This weekend. To Loredo."

Mike came into the sun porch. He was wearing a lavender and pink shirt.

"Oh, hi, Tilly," he said. "What's up?

"Mike! I exclaimed. "Wherever did you get that gay shirt?"

Mike glanced down at his shirt.

"What do you mean 'gay shirt'? I thought you costume designers knew a thing or two about fashion. This is what's 'in' around town."

"Yeah, I said. "It's all the rage in West Hollywood. You'll find those shirts on the guys down at The Abbey and down at Hollywood and Vine at Bob's Frolic Room. And probably the queen of our studio, Karl Tepes, would go wild for it. I suggest you don't wear it down to Olympic Studios. Karl would probably jump your bones."

"I don't believe for a moment that Karl is gay. He's as straight as I am."

I thought he'd hit the nail on the head. Karl was as straight as Mike. I knew that Karl had told Harold Tremaine, one of the best boys at Olympic, that he had a hot date for the weekend. Harold hangs out with some of the girls who work for me and they always gossip about who's doing what to whom. Word got to me about Karl's mystery date. Could it be…?

Mike had not come into the room to talk to me. He hadn't seen me come into the house and was more concerned with getting away to "Loredo" than discussing studio gossip. He turned his attention to Olivia.

"I'm just about all packed, Dear."

"So you're leaving now, Hon?" she replied."

"Yep. I'm picking up Rob at his place over in Larchmont and we'll want to have plenty of time to get to LAX to catch our plane. No big rush, but I'd like to get going within the next half-hour or so."

"Let me come back to the bedroom with you. I have a little going away present," Olivia said.

They smiled that satisfied smirk that goes with approaching intimacies and disappeared into the back of the house.

I sat there in the sun porch thinking about what was going on in the bedroom. Mike was fucking the woman who had turned me on. His hands were gliding over skin that was soft and inviting. His tongue was dancing in and out of that mouth I had kissed so fervently back in our school days. His fingers tripped over rosy nipples that so invited suckling. He was entering into that sweet, warm treasurehouse of delights that dwelt between her thighs. My panties dampened.

"Thou shalt not covet?" I'll tell the world, I was coveting plenty.

I had to have Olivia. My brain kept working on wisps of information that were forming themselves into facts in my mind. I was certain that Mike was lying about flying to Loredo. I became convinced that Mike and Karl had been flirting with each other at work enough to have occasioned at least gossip. Word that Karl was bragging about a hot date for the weekend fit into the emerging picture. And, right in the center of my thought pattern was Olivia's repeated assertion to me. "If I ever found that Mike wandered, I'd be tempted." And her nod to me that she would accompany me to the Eleutheria if she found out he was cheating on her.

Mike was in the bedroom screwing the woman I was steaming for. She could be mine to fuck if I could demonstrate some way that Mike was off on a sex date that very weekend. I sipped my wine cooler and searched for the key. How could I spring the trap?

And I saw a light. The answer was Rob Roberts. There was no way Rob was flying off to Loredo to take pictures with Mike. I doubted that Rob was Mike's date for the weekend. It was of course possible, but I thought it unlikely.

Somehow, if I could induce Rob to call Olivia while Mike was gone… And there I drew a blank. No stratagem came to mind how to convince Rob Roberts to call Olivia.

I'd hit a brick wall so returned my attention to my drink.

I heard the front door open. Someone was entering the house. I got up to see who was intruding and saw Tim come sauntering in.

"Oh, hi, Auntie Til," he bubbled. "I just came by to see Uncle Mike."

"Uncle Mike is busy in the bedroom at the moment," I told him. "Come on into the sun porch with me. He and your Aunt Olivia should be out soon."

Did I tell you about Mike's nephew Tim?

He's a good kid. He was eighteen years old at the time. He'd graduated from Hollywood High School and had been accepted at Stanford. He would be heading up to Palo Alto in the Fall.

He is Mike's brother's son. His family lives on Padre Terrace in Whitley Heights, just a few blocks up from Olivia and Mike. From the time he could safely walk from his place to theirs, he visited his uncle and aunt regularly. And I was with Olivia so often, a kind of fixture at their place, he's always called me Auntie Til.

Tim is a bit of a rascal, but Olivia and Mike think the world of him. And so do I.

From the time Tim was ten, Mike would take him to the studio with him on non-school days. And Tim had the run of the place. He always came to my department and I would take him to the commissary for Cokes and ice cream sundaes. When he was sixteen he began smoking. I don't smoke myself, but I would bum cigarettes off my girls for him. It wasn't too long before he figured out which ones he could go to himself to mooch a smoke. Of course, I never ratted on him to his relatives. We had a kind of bond as partners in crime.

This morning I was talking about, Tim and I were sitting in the sun porch while his uncle and aunt were jazzing it up in the bedroom.

"Whatcha drinking, Auntie Til?"

"Wine cooler. You want one, Tim?"

"Whatdaya think?" he smiled with that smile that serves him so well.

I fixed him a drink and settled down to hear what he was up to.

"You couldn't lend me a few bucks, could you?" he asked.

"I've lent you a few bucks, Tim. And I've learned something about your vocabulary problem."

"Vocabulary problem?"

He knew what I was getting at, but he loves playing the game.

"Yeah, Tim. There's the word 'lend.' To everyone else, it means receiving money from another with the intent to pay it back. When were you thinking of paying me back the fifty dollars I 'lent' you for some emergency or other you claimed to have?"

"This morning," he beamed.

"Great," I said. "Hand it over."

"But first, you have to lend me a hundred fifty bucks. Then, I'll pay you back the fifty I owe you and only owe you a hundred bucks."

"You can con your Uncle Mike. And you can con your Aunt Olivia. You can even con the seamstresses at the studio for your cigarettes. And you can even con me. But with me, you can only do it once. And you've already shot that wad."

"Aw, Auntie Til," he whined. "I know what you think. You think since I'm a teenager, I'm gonna spend the money on drugs. Drugs are for dopes. They fuck up your mind. Alcohol and tobacco, and, oh, yes, caffeine, are the only drugs I'm into. You can trust me on that."

I did, and do, trust the kid to be too smart to get into the drug scene. And in Hollywood, that makes him an exception.

I nodded and took a sip of my cooler.

"How much money were you trying to con me out of, Tim? Sounds like you had me marked for a hundred dollars."

"Bingo! I need a hundred dollars, bad."

"For what evil purpose?"

"Look. I'll be frank with you, Auntie Til. I have a date tonight. And my pockets are empty. I need a little walk-around money."

"Tell me about your date, Big Guy."

"I can tell you, Auntie Til. You're cool. But don't spill the beans to anyone else."

That was a con, of course. I knew it. And I knew he knew it. We both knew I loved to be called 'cool' by that scamp. It was supposed to loosen up the purse strings.

"You know I'll be cool," I told him in the tone of a co-conspirator. "Give."

"Well, there's this gal I met through the studio. She's mature and sophisticated. Named Carol. She goes for me. Says I'm cute and handsome and all."

"She's right about that," I said to give him the ego boost he always enjoys.

"Yeah," he readily agreed. "But I want her to think I'm kinda mature and sophisticated myself. She agreed to see me tonight. So I really, really need some bread in my jeans. Otherwise she'll think I'm only some dumb, broke kid."

"Well?" I joked.

He laughed.

"Carol has an important studio dude as a regular lover. But she likes younger guys, too. She says I'm just her meat."

"What if this 'studio dude' should burst n on you while you are doing your thing with her?"

"Carol says she'll hold him off while I hide. We've got it all worked out."

I wished him luck. I figured he was wily enough to pull off the intrigue.

"Your Uncle Mike will be out here soon. You can usually squeeze him with your sad stories. But, if I were you, I wouldn't try to use the 'I need money to appear sophisticated to my mature date' bit with him.

"Or with your aunt."

I thought he'd probably be successful in sucking a few dollars out of Mike or Olivia. He was good at that. I knew he would do well at Stanford.

Soon Olivia and Mike came sauntering into the room, arm in arm, with post-coital smirks on their faces.

"Hi, Uncle Mike, Aunt Olivia," my junior friend smiled.

"Oh, hi there, Tim," Mike returned. "What's up?"

"I just came by to see my favorite relatives in the whole wide world," Tim schmoozed.

Olivia said, "Your Uncle Mike is about to leave for Loredo. I'm glad you dropped by in time to say goodbye to him."

"Loredo, cool!" Tim said. "Research for that *Showdown* movie, huh?"

"You got it, Sport," Mike said with pride.

"Before you go, could you manage to lend me a little something?" Tim asked.

"Probably," Mike bit. "How much do you need?"

"I could really use a hundred bucks," Tim ventured.

I leaned back to watch the young rogue operate. I really enjoy his shenanigans.

"A hundred bucks!" Mike blurted. "I thought you said a 'little' something."

Olivia was a somewhat softer touch than Mike and intervened.

"Now, Mike," she chimed in. "Listen to what Tim has to say. He probably has a good reason for needing the money."

"All right," Mike agreed. "Just why in the world would a young man like you need so much money at one time?"

I knew the answer. And I knew there was no way Tim would give them the real answer. So I waited eagerly to see what he would come up with.

"For San Francisco," he said, a touch of hopefulness in his voice.

"That is not exactly an answer to my question," Mike said patiently.

"Sure it is, Uncle Mike," Tim answered, warming up to his pitch.

"You know Palo Alto's just down the Peninsula from San Francisco."

"Thank you for the geography lesson," Mike smiled.

"Now let's hear him out," Olivia suggested.

Tim shot his warmest smile at her.

"When I get to Stanford, all the guys from the Bay Area will already know all about San Francisco."

"Know all *what* about San Francisco?" Mike challenged.

"All the cultural sites. I'll look like a hick from Hicksville if I don't know anything about anything in San Francisco."

"Hollywood – Los Angeles – Beverly Hills – Here? *This* is Hicksville?"

Mike exclaimed.

I scored one for Mike. He wasn't making it easy for his nephew.

"What places in San Francisco do you want to see?" Olivia asked. She was clearly on Tim's side.

Tim gulped. He had come on this raid of his uncle's wallet without having done sufficient research.

I could help him out at that point. And I was rooting for him to worm the money from Mike.

I happen to know Frisco quite well. For years I had gone up there the last week in June for the Lesbian-Gay-Bisexual-Transgender Pride Celebration. It's number one in the world and only four hundred miles or so north of Hollywood. I have contacts there with a number of the sisters. And I get in more loving in one week there than in a month at home. That week in Frisco is party time plus.

But I always manage to include some work when I'm in Frisco. I get to a few museums with my sketch pads and make drawings of costumes to bring back to the studio. It's not as much fun, maybe, as fucking. But it's an extra pleasure I throw into the pot. And now I could use that experience to bolster Tim's scam.

"Tim and I were discussing that while you two were busy in the bedroom." I said with a degree of evil innuendo.

"He's been studying the cultural aspects of the Bay Area. He wants to visit the De Young Museum to take in the classic and impressionistic exhibit there. I suggested the San Francisco Museum of Modern art, and he got pretty excited about it. The Asian Art Museum is one he seems most excited about. And what was it you were telling me about, Tim? Oh, yes. The Legion of Honor. I've visited it but you're way ahead of me in your interest in the exhibit at the California Academy of Sciences and the Steinhart Aquarium."

"Oh, yes, Auntie Til," he ventured in confidently. "Those are on the list they sent me from Stanford about the places they want us students to visit before classes start."

"I think we should help him, Darling," Olivia said to Mike.

Definitely a soft touch. I was wishing I could touch her as well to satisfy my own horny needs.

"If it's that important, your father will probably give you the money," Mike said.

"You know how dad is," Tim sighed. "He's not all sold on culture like you are. I asked him, and he said I should go earn the money if it's so important to me. Where am I gonna get a job between now and September? Oh, Uncle

Mike! Aunt Olivia! I really want to do well up there at Stanford. And a measly hundred bucks would make all the difference in the world."

I could see them both melt. It was Olivia, of course, who stated it first.

"Oh, Mike. Tim is *so* right. That's not an awful lot of money for us. And it could change his whole life to take in those cultural places in San Francisco."

"All right," Mike grumbled. But with a decidedly avuncular grumble.

He pulled out his wallet and peeled off a couple of fifty dollar bills. He handed them over to his nephew.

"See that you spend that in the right places," he cautioned.

"Oh, believe me, Uncle Mike. I will."

I know the lad would have winked at me if he had dared.

He shook Mike's hand, hugged Olivia, waved at me and excused himself to go to the library to check out books on the required reading list from the university. I bet!

Mike went to get his overnight bag, kissed Olivia goodbye, gave me a peck on the cheek, and he was off on his adventure.

I needed to get away myself. My task was to find a way to get Olivia and Rob together while Mike was off to his tryst somewhere. I needed some peace and quiet to crack that nut.

By the time I got in my Beemer, Mike's Mountaineer was already out of sight and I saw Tim's skateboard rounding the corner.

When I reached the corner, I saw a sight that nearly caused me to have an accident. It was a deep blue-colored 1967 Corvette convertible, with the top down. That car is as well-known to Hollywood insiders as the Pantages Theater. I knew who was driving it without having to look at who was behind the wheel. Rob Roberts was driving up Franklin in the opposite direction from me. I recognized him and his vintage car and doubted he would know my car by sight. He passed right by me and pulled up in front of Olivia's place.

Out of the clear blue sky the answer to my hopes seemed to appear. I pulled over to the curb and watched through my rearview and sideview mirrors. I was one happy voyeuse.

Rob got out of his 'Vette and went up the sidewalk to Olivia's place. He was carrying a kind of attaché case.

He rang the bell. The door opened and Rob entered.

Too good to be true? In my lifetime there have been exactly three times that timing defied the laws of probability. This was one of them.

I continued to watch the door to that house as though mesmerized. Five minutes passed. Eight minutes passed. My watch ticked off the minutes all too slowly.

Nine minutes after he entered the house, I saw Rob come out the door. He still carried that attaché case. He got in his car and shot up the road as only a real driving enthusiast can.

When he disappeared down Cherokee, I whipped my car around and went back to Olivia's.

I rang the bell with trembling fingers.

When Olivia answered the door, she was visibly shaken. I entered the livingroom.

"I was just driving away when I saw Rob Roberts' 'Vette pull up in front of your place," I said. "I came back to see if he mentioned anything about Tuesday's staff meeting that I should know about."

"I need a drink," Olivia said.

She went to the wetbar in the room and poured us each a healthy shot of Chivas over some ice cubes.

"What's the matter, Dear?" I asked. Knowing perfectly well what was the matter.

"That was Rob," she said, and dropped down onto the sofa. I sat beside her.

"Yes, I know," I said.

(I thought we had already established that fact.)

"He brought by a packet of photos for Mike to look over before your staff meeting next week. They're in that envelope on the coffee table."

I didn't press her. She was trying to cope with the implications.

"He said for Mike to call him at his place on Larchmont if he had any questions or new ideas."

I sipped my Scotch with a thrill of satisfaction.

I put my arm across her shoulders.

"Which means?" I prompted.

"That Mike's lying to me."

"I'm so sorry," I lied.

She burst into tears and I hugged her close.

I didn't go in for the kill right away. I sympathized. I plied her with Chivas. I got Kleenex for her to wipe away her tears.

The more she drank, the more resolute she grew in her determination to "get" Mike for this.

I agreed with her, but did not push the point yet. I let her come to a conclusion by herself.

"You know what I'll do?" she asked.

"I can't imagine."

"I've told you before, Tilly, that I'd go off to your Eleutheria if I ever found out that rat was cheating on me."

"I know."

"I have to admit that I've been curious about what lesbian lovemaking would be like. To tell you the truth, I've really been attracted to you that way for a long time."

"Me, too."

"I really want to," she insisted.

"Let me call Madame Alexander at the Eleutheria," I said. "I'll reserve a room for us right now."

Through her tears Olivia said, "Go ahead. I'm ready. I want to have forbidden sex at the same time that louse is having his."

I called Madame Alexander and made the arrangements.

My dream had come true. Olivia would be in my arms in a matter of hours.

CHAPTER TWO
AS TOLD BY OLIVIA AXELROD

There's a sordid little story about my lying husband Mike. Tilly's probably told you about it. Because of his lies I'd agreed to go to the Eleutheria with my oldest and best friend.

Tilly picked me up at my place on Franklin over by Whitley Heights in her Beemer in the late afternoon. I'd only packed some undies, toiletries and cosmetics because Tilly was bringing costumes for us. She'd also told me to bring along a pair of black or red boots. I brought a pair of each.

We headed for Villa Eleutheria which, I guess, is usually just called The Eleutheria or even Eleutheria without any "The" in front of it. It's named after some kind of party the Greeks used to hold to honor Eros, the god of love. Whatever.

What it is, is a kind of hostel for lovers. Particularly gays, lesbians, sado-masochists, and all that. In other words, non-straights. I'd heard about it even back when I was attending Hollywood High.

She drove east to Beachwood and then we twisted and turned up into the Hollywood Hills until I lost all sense of where we were. I noticed Ridgerton Drive along the way but couldn't tell you any of the streets beyond that. The

Eleutheria was located behind a gated wall with a callbox. Tilly called through, the gate opened, and we entered.

The place had no sign of any kind. There were several parking spaces that were fenced off so no one coming in could see your car. I guess that's for anonymity freaks. We took our things out of the Beemer, closed off the car privacy gate, and entered the lobby.

Madame Alexander, the concierge, greeted us and directed us to our room.

The rooms at Eleutheria are customized to the taste of the individual guests. Some clients request chains, whips, manacles, etc. Others want an assortment of erotic toys. Madame Alexander had arranged for our room to be dominated by an enormous heart-shaped bed with pink sheets and covers and a wild assortment of black pillows, cushions, and bolsters. On the walls were some fifty or so pictures that were in the style of paintings on Grecian urns. Each picture featured two or more women engaged in sex acts. I studied the pictures and convinced myself that the human body could not possibly contort itself into some of those uncomfortable positions.

In one corner was a wet bar. I checked out the liquors. There were three bottles of Grey Goose Orange vodka, two bottles of Cointreau, four bottles of Rose's lime juice, a half-dozen Mexican limes, and a gallon of cranberry juice. No pre-mixed Cosmopolitan cocktails for us. A Hollywood Cosmo has to be mixed fresh each time. When you come to Hollywood, the only thing you really need to know is how to mix a Cosmo.

(Into a cocktail shaker containing ice, pour two parts Grey Goose Orange and one part each Cointreau, Rose's, and cranberry juice. Shake but do not bruise. Strain into Martini glass, garnish with lime wedge.)

(Do not commit the faux pas of adding lemon zest as they do in Beverly Hills or Curaçao as they do in Culver City. You won't be invited back if you do.)

On the bed Tilly placed the box that contained our costumes. She had created harlequin masks for each of us. The masks were black and festooned with pink feathers arranged in concentric circles around the eye-holes. The rest of the costume consisted of a large satin cape for each of us. The capes were black on one side and pink on the other. They were large enough to wrap around the whole body, but designed to be worn draped over the shoulders in such a way as to display full frontal nudity if desired. The ensemble to be accessorized by black or red boots.

Tilly led me to the exterior door where we gazed out at the deck. It is cantilevered out over the hillside, and features a swimming pool and spa. There are various styles of deck chairs, divans, chaises longues, cushions, and mats strewn around. We stepped out to admire the view of all Hollywood sparkling up at us from the plain below. Breathtaking!

We went back into the room, stripped, and laid aside our capes, masks and boots for later.

Tilly mixed the Cosmos and we stretched out languidly on the heart-shaped bed, bolstered by enormous black pillows.

"Do you remember how we practiced kissing back in high school?" Tilly asked.

"Um-humm!"

"Those kisses weren't flavored with Cosmos," she hummed.

"I'll bet we were missing something," I hazarded.

"Let's see," she challenged.

We each took a fair sized sip of cocktail, kept it in our mouths, set our glasses down on the side tables, and joined lips.

We exchanged the lovely liquors back and forth from one mouth to another. Our tongue-play was Cosmo flavored. Another sip, another juicy kiss, an entangling of tongues. We finished off our cocktails with constant delicious kisses.

I got out of bed and mixed the next batch.

This was more exciting than any sex I had had with Mike in years. Our Wednesday and Friday unimaginative sex had, frankly, become routine and boring. And I'll admit that I had fantasized about having really exciting sex with Tilly for quite a long time.

By the time we'd finished the second batch of Cosmos, I was drenched in my cunt.

Tilly suggested I slip down spread-eagle on the bed and let her entertain me. I was more than ready to be entertained.

She began by lavishing kitten-kisses all over my face. Little lappings of the tongue that made me giggle, shiver, and mew. She settled her tongue on my left earlobe and played circles around the ear orifice itself. I told her to desist, but didn't mean it. And she knew I didn't mean it.

She nuzzled my neck, and new sensations coursed up and down my body, causing pleasant contractions in my pussy.

Her hands encircled my tits, making those circular motions her tongue had drawn on my ear. When her fingers circled around my nipples I could feel them grow tingly rigid.

As Tilly's lips worked my turgid nipples, a thought lingered in the back of my mind. "In all the years Mike and I had made love, how did it happen that he never pleasured my body like this?"

Her lips, tongue, hands, and fingers worked their way down my body slowly, sensuously, surely. There was no mistaking their destination.

When she arrived at my labia, my clit was pulsating. Somehow I could bear the tension no longer.

"Now!" I whispered frantically. "I have to come, Tilly. Help me!"

She sucked sweetly on the throbbing nub that had emerged from its hood and was demanding succor.

Tilly licked and sucked at my jewel until suddenly my body arched and wracked into an overwhelming orgasm such as I had never experienced before. I was drenched with sweat and with the sweet nectars that flowed out of my cunt and coated my thighs.

Strange to say, Tilly seemed as excited and as happy about my grand release as I was. It had never been like that in the marriage bed.

When I recovered from the spasms, I asked Tilly if she wanted me to do similar things to her body.

"No, my dear," she answered. "The pleasure you have given me in allowing me to pleasure you is enough for now. When the time comes that you spontaneously want to make love to me, not in response to anything I have done to you, I will be ready."

That kind of unselfish giving of carnal love was new to me. What I was experiencing was not sex, but Love

We were both covered with sweat and went to the bathroom to shower together. I took the lead in lathering her tits and cunt. It wasn't an act prompted by her lovemaking to me. I did it for the pleasure of running my hands over those glorious erogenous zones. I did not wish to carry the action further than that at the time. Nor, clearly, did Tilly expect me to.

Showered and refreshed, we thought it was time to enjoy another Cosmo. I took the initiative in bartending while Tilly spread out our masks and capes on the bed. She set our boots on the side of the bed and placed her black ones beside my red ones.

We donned our masks, capes, and boots and sat in the two overstuffed chairs that were next to the cocktail table.

Caped, masked, and shod, with pinkish drinks in hand, we clinked glasses and laughed giddily.

When we had drained our glasses, I asked, "What next?"

"We go out onto the deck."

"Like this?"

"Like this."

"What if anyone sees us?"

"Who?"

I couldn't answer.

Tilly said, "We can't be seen from the street or from the neighboring houses. Only by people who are staying here as guests. And I would guess they are pretty open-minded."

I laughed.

"Let's go!"

And out we went to enjoy the freedom of being masked and caped, in the open air, under the moon and stars, with the lights of our beloved Hollywood twinkling up at us.

The soft, warm breeze flowed over us, causing our satin capes to billow gently behind us. The feel of the air over my nude knockers and bush was like a caress of Nature. We stood at the overlook fence, suspended out over the hillside on the cantilevered deck. I had never felt more free, more liberated, or more content any previous moment in my life.

I put my arm around Tilly's bare waist and guided her to a chaise longue that had been placed close to the overlook fence. She complied with the silent direction I was giving her. When we got to the edge of the chaise I simply nodded at it. Tilly reclined on the piece in the mode of an odalisque. I untied the cape cord at her neck so she was lying totally uncovered. The cape spread beneath her was pink-side up. The full moon lowered gentle beams onto the soft whiteness of her body reclining on that satiny-pink background. It was the most erotic sight I had ever seen.

I lovingly removed her mask from her face and then took off my own. I wanted every kissable surface of skin to be exposed for my hungering lips and fingers.

I gathered a near-by cushion and placed it beside the chaise longue. I sank to my knees on the cushion, leaned over my lesbian lover and encircled her mouth with my own. As we tangled and jostled tongues, I rested one hand on her midriff and ran the fingers of the other hand through her hair in loving caresses.

With the hand that had landed on her abdomen I traced patterns from her tits to the top of her bush. I kept my touch as soft as gossamer. The messages our tongues exchanged were expressions of Aphrodite and her naughty son Eros.

For the first time in my life I was making love. This was nothing like "having sex." I was engaged in the mystic and mythic celebration of the Eleutheria as it must have been experienced three millennia ago.

My lips insisted on sucking those hooters that my hand had fondled to a state of arousal. As I closed my lips over those nipples, I released my one hand from her hair and traced circles around her lips with a finger. She extended her lips around my thumb and sucked on it lasciviously. My other hand descended from her bush to her cunt. I played with its moist lips and then gently inserted my thumb past those outer lips just about a half inch into her hole. I coordinated my in-and-out- movements there with the rhythm she set in sucking my thumb.

I was suddenly aware that our lovemaking was being observed by the moon and the stars above. And even, I hoped, by fellow guests at the villa from their windows. This was primal. It was the expression of every celebration of the glorious gift of Love as practiced by devotees of the Goddess from the Eleutherian mysteries to Lughnasa. In the open air of the Hollywood Hills, Tilly and I had become one with the Goddess, urged on by her naughty son with his benign bow and arrows.

The fragrant nectar that flowed over my thumb urgently attracted my salivating mouth. Sweeter than honey. Sweeter than a Hollywood Cosmo, its perfume called me to sip from the banks of Lethe.

I bent my lips to her waiting cunt. I drank. I licked. I quaffed. I became drunk on her excrescence of Aphrodite.

When she shuddered in ecstasy, a sense of elation filled my entire body as I raised my lips to hers and kissed her deeply as my fingers played soft tattoos across her love bud.

Despite my perspiration drenched body, or perhaps because of it, I felt a refreshing chill envelope me.

With no need for words, I looked into her eyes and our deep stares exchanged the unspoken words that each of us understood.

I arose from the cushion under my knees, touched her cheek and returned her mask to her. We each put on our feathered masks again.

I wrapped my satin cape around my trembling body and returned to our room. I needed to lie there in the heart-shaped bed and absorb the exquisite experience that had been granted to me beneath the moon-drenched and star-spangled sky.

Tilly remained on the deck, free to relax into her own reminiscence of the love act we had engaged in.

CHAPTER THREE
AS TOLD BY TILLY BLAINE

I shall not attempt to describe the lovemaking between my darling and me in our first hour at The Eleutheria. I had waited for that hour for more years than I care to count. From our "practice kisses" as teenagers to its consummation in the magic ambiance of our beloved Hollywood Hills.

I was lying on a chaise longue on the deck of The Eleutheria filled with a satisfaction that surpassed all previous lovemaking. I arose from the chaise, leaving my cape stretched over its surface with its satiny-pink hues reflecting the sacred moonlight. With my mask covering the top half of my face I glided over to the hot tub and lowered my tingling body into the gurgling, bubbling hot water.

I laid my head on the edge of the spa, facing the smiling moon overhead.

I don't know how long I gloried there in the soothing waters, lost in replays of the worship my love and I had rendered to the Goddess. I may have been thus dreaming for five minutes or a half-hour. Perhaps more. Time had very little meaning.

But a length, I was aware of another body lowering itself into the bubbling waters. A quick glance revealed that the naked body sharing the waters was decidedly male.

I felt no compunction against looking directly at him from behind the anonymity of my mask.

What a shock! What a delight!

My companion in the spa was none other than Mike Axelrod, my longstanding friend and the husband of my lesbian lover.

He felt my eyes exploring his face. His body was submerged in the hot, effervescent water. I didn't need to explore his soaking male body. He did not spend much time considering the face hidden behind a pink-feathered harlequin mask. He leaned his head back on the spa edge, looked for a while at the starry sky, sighed, and closed his eyes.

I didn't leave the tub immediately. I didn't want him to think he had driven me away. He might have felt he should say something stupid and chivalrous. Besides, I enjoyed having time to gloat to myself.

At length, I quietly slipped out of the water, went to the chaise longue, retrieved my cape, and returned to our room. I removed my mask and draped my cape over a chair. I stretched out on the bed beside my lover.

She took my hand in hers and gave it a gentle squeeze.

"That was the most glorious moment in my entire life," she confided.

"Mine, too."

"I love you, Tilly."

The words thrilled me beyond measure.

"And I have loved you since we were children," I returned.

I just lay there next to her, holding her hand, and enjoying feeling of great contentment.

When I thought the moment pregnant, I broached the next subject.

"After you returned to the room," I said. "I went for a dip in the hot tub."

"How's the water temperature?" she asked.

"Just the way I like it. Very warm but not overly hot. It's not one of those whirlpools that practically boil you. Perfect."

We lay there silently breathing, enjoying the nearness of our bodies. When I felt the moment was right, I said, "Someone came out onto the deck and joined me in the tub."

"Man or woman?" came the expected reply.

"A man. I was masked so there was no way he could tell who I was. But I could see perfectly well who he was."

She stirred in interest.

"Anyone famous?"

"Depends on what you mean by famous. Not a well-known actor or celebrity of that type. But well-known in some circles."

"Really? Who?"

"He's a set designer."

Olivia sat bolt upright.

"At Olympic Studios?" she exclaimed.

"As a matter of fact."

"Not Mike?"

"You got it, Baby. Your husband who was supposedly off to Loredo is soaking his ass out there in the tub on the deck."

"That louse!"

She said she wanted to go right out there to confront him. But I had a better idea, and explained it to her.

I suggested we go out onto the deck in our costumes. There are floor mats on the deck. What I thought we should do was pull a couple of mats up close to the spa. And, keeping our masks on, I suggested we make lesbian love in front of his startled, and probably amused, eyes.

"Talk about revenge!" Olivia enthused. "That's exactly what I want to do."

So we got out of the bed, donned masks and capes, and marched out onto the deck.

We gathered up a couple of mats and quite deliberately placed them directly within Mike's line of vision. We removed our capes and laid them carefully beneath us on the mats.

I lay down north to south and she stretched herself out parallel with me. Our faces were next to each other, our legs extended. One of the prints on the wall of our room represented two Fifth Century Greek Lesbians in just such a position. It was up to us to fancy our moves from that setting.

Our lips met in a deep, satisfying kiss. Moonlight illuminated our nude bodies.

The air was electric. We were positive that Mike was watching us in rapt attention. Knowing that he was watching us was a gigantic turn-on. Delicious!

So began another session of love in the moonlight. With the added thrill of being objects of attention by a voyeur.

As we kissed, our hands caressed each other's body. And, both inspired by the same idea, we explored the other's cunt with one hand while pleasuring ourselves below with the other. That would surely get Mike's horny attention.

When we had kissed enough, and masturbated enough, we slid in opposite directions, so we were mouth to breast. We made our suckling loud enough to carry over the sounds of the bubbling tub our observer was sitting in.

Another slithering of our bodies and we were tongue to navel. We were still in position so that I had one finger sliding up and down Olivia's cunt-lips and one pleasuring my own koozie. Olivia followed my lead. This was so satisfying that I, for one, forgot all about our voyeuristic friend for a moment. When I did think about him, I hoped he was also jacking off. There was no way to tell, because we never looked in his direction.

At length, we scooted farther, so we could kiss each other's pussies. We spent considerable noisy time tonguing each other. We got a good mouth purchase on each other's clit at the same time. We orgasmed simultaneously, with loud, satisfying sighs.

We then arose from our mats, put our capes back on, and returned to our room.

We were sure that Mike did not recognize who we were.

After the return to our room, we quietly crept back out onto the deck and hid in the shadows to watch and see what Mike would do next.

CHAPTER FOUR

AS TOLD BY TIM AXELROD

Uh, Hi! I'm Tim. And what I'm gonna tell you here is just between us. Okay? So be cool.

I was eighteen when this stuff happened at a place up in the Hills. It opened my eyes to a lotta stuff that's helped me since. So I'll tell you 'cause it just might help you, too.

I'd graduated from Hollywood High with good grades. And I did fine in my SATs. Besides, my dad and grad-dad are both Stanford alumni. So, with one thing and another, I'd been accepted at Stanford and was kinda kicking back that summer before heading off to Palo Alto.

Frankly, at the time, I was confused about sex. Oh, sure. In school there was a segment in science class called "Family Life Education." That was the name they gave to sex education at the time. It was everything you didn't care to know about sex. I never knew anyone to get a hardon from "Family Life Education." And for teenage guys, if it doesn't give you a hardon, it's not really about sex. And who needs to know more about "family life"?

What did I know?

First and foremost, at age eighteen, I mostly knew about wet dreams and jacking off. I was always checking out the chicks and comparing notes with my buddies about Gloria's legs, Dottie's tits, and Marilou's ass. Which chick you'd most want to kiss, feel, or fuck. And we'd lie about who we'd felt up or nailed. Lots and lots of bullshit.

I'd never gotten beyond second base with any of the gals. Even though I had the distinct advantage of having a car. True, it was a Honda Civic. It would require a couple of gymnasts to really get it on in that car. Probably why it was the car my folks bought for me. But it did enable me to drive chicks up to Mulholland Drive and get my hands on a few boobies and once I got a hand job from a chick in our class, Fanny, who didn't get too many dates without at least putting out to that degree.

But it wasn't only chicks I dug. I was very interested in the dudes, too. Muscles held a strong attraction. In the gym showers I'd memorized the dongs of every hip dude in class and when I was jacking off I'd fantasize in that direction just about as often as in the direction of tits, snatch, and asses.

My buddy Bob and I had engaged in mutual jackoff probably a dozen times as teenagers. That was as close to homosexuality as I got. It wasn't really much of a big deal. More like a sport than an erotic experience.

All this is by way of saying that despite "sex education," bullshit with the guys, groping and being groped, and extensive lovemaking to my fist, I was really one confused idiot about sex.

Was I gay? Was I straight? That was the question I was wrestling with. What I wanted to be was straight. That's what I thought I really was. But I wasn't sure. Like I say, I was confused.

One thing I knew. I really wanted to make it with a chick. I thought once I'd lost my cherry I would really be a man. And I would have established a definite heterosexual orientation once and for all. I didn't think I needed to get it on with Brad Cole, the stud muffin who was our quarterback, to see how I liked that. But, I've gotta admit I did fantasize a few times about him sucking my dick.

But most of all, I wanted to get it on with a woman. Preferably a mature one who would know what she was doing and would initiate me into the real mysteries of sex.

And that's where Carol came in.

My Uncle Mike is a really good guy. He works as a hotshot set designer over at Olympic Studios. From the time I was ten or eleven years old, he would take me with him to the Studios on Saturdays or when I had a school holiday.

Lots of people who worked at Olympic got to know me. I never got in their way and Uncle Mike's friends went out of their way to let me see a scene being shot or an actor being made up for a part. That sort of thing.

Uncle Mike and Aunt Olivia had a real good friend who's a costume designer at Olympic. She wasn't any kind of real relative, but I'd always called her Auntie Til. She was always a real pal to me. She'd take me to the commissary and she'd slip me cigs, even though she doesn't smoke herself. A real friend. So people she knew at the studio were real nice and friendly to me too.

Otto Caruthers, the famous director, let me hang around the sets for *Vampires at the O.K. Corral.* I *really* loved that. All the actors and actresses were either in vampire makeup and costumes or decked out as cowboys and saloongirls. Everyone always seemed to be having a good time when they were shooting that movie. It's still my fav pic of all time.

One of the actors in that movie was Karl Tepes.

You might not recognize his name but you've seen him in dozens of movies. In movies about the Mafia, he's always one of the creepy guys who are never up to good. He was even in that comedy *Kids Rule* as the little kid's step-dad. His voice is different in every part he plays. So you might not recognize him beneath the makeup and the voice he's using. But I know you've seen Karl Tepes if you've been to more than three Olympic pictures in the past five years or so.

I was sitting on the floor behind the cameraman when they were shooting that scene where that bunch of vampires all rise from their coffins at the same time and head for the house by the lake.

Mr. Caruthers was satisfied with how the shoot went and told the cast to take a break and come back at two. Mr. Tepes walked over to where I was sitting.

"Hi, Kid," he said. "What did you think of the scene?"

I stood up, of course. The guy was in his full vampire regalia and I thought it was about as cool as cool could be to stand there talking to a vampire. And to be asked by him for a critique of a scene.

"It'll scare the heck out of everyone who sees it," I answered.

"You have the eye of a critic," he said.

I basked in his vampire smile.

"You're Mike Axelrod's relative," he said. It was a statement, not a question.

I nodded, having no clever response to make.

"How old are you?"

"Eighteen."

"Eighteen," he mused. "You've practically grown up here at Olympic, haven't you?"

"Yeah," I agreed. "Kinda."

"I've got a secret for you. Can you keep a secret?"

The Vampire's Secret. It sounded more like a movie title than anything related to reality.

"I'm the best darned secret keeper in the world," I bragged.

I was really proud of that answer. I thought it sounded kinda sophisticated and grown up.

"There's a lady in the cosmetics department named Carol. She's the one who put this vampire makeup on me. Pretty good job, isn't it?"

"She really made you scary looking, Mr. Tepes."

"Thank you," he said.

We both laughed. I wasn't really nervous around him now. He wasn't only a good actor. It turned out he was a good, friendly guy. And he had a secret to tell me. Something about makeup. I was super-intrigued.

"This Carol babe, she's noticed you around the studio."

"Yeah?"

"Just this morning, while she was doing my face and adjusting my fangs, she mentioned you to me."

This was turning into the most interesting conversation I'd ever had in my life. *Conversation with a Vampire.* A conversation that was turning out to be about me. I didn't know what to say. I felt like I might be blushing.

Mr. Tepes picked up the slack in the discussion.

"Would you like to know what she said to me?"

"Sure," I stammered.

"She told me she thinks you're cute. What do you think of that?"

I answered truthfully.

"I don't know."

"She said she likes guys about your age. She says you turn her on. I envy you, Kid. I wish I turned Carol on. But to her I'm only a face to slap makeup and fangs on. I've tried to put the make on her myself. No soap. She's attracted to younger men. And you know what?"

"What?"

"She'd like to meet you. She told me so herself."

I wanted to say something like "Holy shit" But I couldn't express anything more than, "She did?"

"She's a mature woman. Great shape. A voluptuous mouth. Knockers to drool for. Would you like to meet her?"

Would I? She sounded like the answer to some of my wettest dreams.

But all I could say was, "Yeah. I guess so."

Mr. Tepes looked at his watch.

"Look, Kid," he said. "It's eleven o'clock now. I'll be knocking off here for a while. I'm going into town for lunch and my dressing room will be free. I'll give Carol a key to the room and tell her she can use it during lunch break. Would you like to meet her there at noon?"

I nearly wet my pants. I got the shakes. I couldn't help myself. A mature woman who said I turned her on. A chance to meet her in private. What eighteen-year-old could refuse a deal like that?

"Sure," I said.

"You know where my dressing room is?" he asked.

I knew where the dressing rooms were. I knew his name would be on a door there. I would have no trouble finding it.

"I can find it," I assured him.

"I'll tell Carol," he smiled with a smile that was in character. "Don't stand her up now, Kid. Noon at my dressing room."

"I'll be there," I said.

He gave me a playful punch on my arm and went away whistling softly.

"High noon," I thought. "A man's gotta do what a man's gotta do."

I found Uncle Mike and told him I was going to the commissary for an early lunch and wanted to go over and watch a shoot of *The Mad Lover of Notre-Dame* scheduled for noon on Lot B.

He said "fine." And we planned to meet at three o'clock at his office.

I went to the commissary for a burger and a Coke.

I could hardly wait for noon.

At the prick of noon I approached the door. It did not have a star on it. Karl was not, and would never be, a star. A very accomplished actor? Yes. Star? Not the way Hollywood bestows that title on box office draws who stand before cameras with or without talent.

The name was on the door. Karl Tepes. Surely a screen name. I knew enough about the Dracula legend to know where he'd cribbed that name. You'd be surprised how many of us in Hollywood, kids and adults alike, are into that vampire and monsters shit.

I knocked on the door with trepidation. I really did not know where this adventure would be heading. I nearly wanted to back out. But I wanted to proceed even more.

Knock, knock.

A sultry, sexy, female voice responded.

"Come in."

When I stepped in, the first thing I glommed onto with my eyes was her face. It was heavily made up. Of course. Makeup was her business.

A pretty face. Not beautiful, but certainly pretty. She was about the age of my folks, I guessed. Maybe a little younger. Long, flowing blond hair. Green eyes. Rosebud mouth.

I dropped my glance to her chest. Stacked. Yes, Karl had said she had knockers to drool for. I could feel my mouth fill with spit.

She was sitting on a three-legged stool with her legs crossed. Better than average gams.

In short, she was better than any chick I'd dated. Just more mature. And to my mind, that was a plus, too.

"Come on the rest of the way in and close the door, Tim. You're delicious. But I promise not to bite."

There was magic, sensuality, and seduction in that voice. I was in love.

I closed the door.

"I'm Carol, Tim," she said. "I've had my eye on you for a long time. I'm glad you came to visit me."

"Yes, Ma'am," I sputtered.

"That's 'Yes, Carol,' Darling. I feel you and I are going to be great friends."

I was able to get out a line that I thought was pretty mature.

"I certainly hope so, Carol."

"Do you like girls, Tim?" she asked.

"Uh-huh."

Not too cool, that answer. This was new territory for me and I knew she could tell I was struggling. But I thought she kinda dug the way I was acting and I started to relax a bit.

"Come over here, Tim," she coaxed. "Do you like to be called 'Tim' or 'Timmy'?"

"Tim," I said. My voice kinda cracked a little but she pretended not to notice.

"How many girls have you kissed, Tim?" she asked.

"Oh, lots," I lied

"How about more mature women?"

"Not as many," I said.

That, at least, was the truth.

She stood up. She was just about my height. A little taller than most of the girls I knew.

"Would you like to show me how you kiss?" she asked.

"I guess so," I answered.

Damn! What a lame answer. She didn't make fun of it, though.

She pulled me to her. Those great boobs pressed against my chest. She pulled my head to hers and our lips met. She took the initiative of sliding her tongue into my mouth. When I reciprocated…yikes! She reached down and gently grabbed me by the nuts. I actually had to hold back a scream.

I was hard as a rock, of course. She ran her hand up and down the outline of my dick.

She receded out of our kiss.

"My, my, Tim," she said. "You are quite a man down there. Would you mind if I checked out the merchandise?"

I've gotta admit. I was really embarrassed. Sure, I'd gotten that hand job from Fanny when we were necking up on Mulholland. But I'd had to kind of coax her to do it. And I was even a little embarrassed back then at exposing my cock to a girl. But this! Wow!!

Carol didn't wait for me to answer. She sat back down on that stool and unbuckled my belt. I just stood there in front of her like some kind of fool. But, to tell the truth, a very happy and excited fool.

She unbuttoned my pants with an expertise that suggested she'd been in this neighborhood before.

My pants slipped to the floor. She pulled my jockey shorts out so they wouldn't snag on my boner and she slipped them down so they met my pants.

"Did you know you have a gorgeous penis, Tim?" she asked.

I didn't know whether the right answer to that was 'yes' or 'no.' So I just swallowed the load of spit that filled my mouth.

"That penis is *so* big," she continued.

I knew that wasn't really the truth. I'd been comparing my dick with those of all the other guys in the gym showers since junior high. And I'd held my friend Bob's hard cock in my hand and had jacked him off a few times. Mine wasn't any bigger than any other cock, and smaller than some.

But, true or not, I loved having her say my prick was "*so* big."

"I just can't resist it," Carol said. "I have to taste that young, virile, magnificent phallus," she said.

"Phallus?" I'd read the word before, but always thought of it as belonging to gods or statues or something. Not a matter to ponder, though, at the time.

She wrapped that rosebud mouth around my cockhead. She took one suck, and I knew I was gonna come right away. Would I spoil it all if I came into her mouth?

Before I could resolve the issue, I shot my wad right into her mouth. She didn't gag or anything. But instead took my balls into one hand, sucked the top of my dick with her mouth, and rubbed my shaft up and down with her other hand, milking it of every drop I thought I had in me.

"That was very nice, Tim," she said when she'd swallowed my cum. "Did you like it?"

"Oh, Boy!" I blurted.

I didn't think at all. The answer just burst out like that.

She reached to the table behind her and picked up a kind of towel.

"Here, Tim," she said. "You'll want to wipe off that powerful weapon you've got there before you pull your pants back up."

I took the towel, cleaned myself up, and got my shorts and pants back on.

While I was cleaning up, I turned away from her, modestly, to wipe off my dick. I realize how ridiculous that was. She had just sucked my cock and swallowed my cum. And I was too modest to let her see me cleaning myself off. My modesty was foolish, I knew. But I couldn't bring myself to stand there in front of a female while I cleaned off my dong. I'm not sure I could do so even today. Go figure!

When I was tidied up and re-clothed, she asked me to sit down on a nearby chair.

"Look, Tim," she said. "I know I could show you a really good time. Not just a quick fellatio at noon."

"Fellatio." Now there was a word like "phallus." A word you read but don't say. What was with this broad? She didn't call cocksucking "cocksucking" but "fellatio." I bet she didn't call a hardon a "hardon" but a phallus. Maybe that's the way adults talk, I thought. Or perhaps just sophisticated adults. I hoped I would be a sophisticated adult at Stanford so I had a lot to learn. Maybe I'd even start saying coitus instead of "fucking."

All this passed through my mind in a flash. I didn't miss a word of what she was saying. I was all ears.

"Do you have a car?" she asked.

"Yeah," I said.

"Terrific! Would you be able to get away tomorrow evening about six?"

I thought for a moment. I could always tell my folks I had a date with a girl. No problem.

"Sure," I said confidently.

This sounded like it was gonna be pretty exciting, whatever it was she had in mind.

"What I'm gong to suggest has a little risk," she said. "I know you have...balls."

She smiled and I know I blushed.

"It'll take balls," she continued. "But I think you might find it fun."

She paused and I leaned forward to see what she was going to suggest that could possibly be more fun than getting your cock sucked at noon at a movie studio. It would *have* to be something pretty terrific.

"Tomorrow evening I have a date with a boyfriend. He's my age, not yours. We'll be up in the Hills. At the Eleutheria. Ever hear of it?"

I told her I had heard of it but didn't know exactly where it was.

"When my boyfriend goes there to meet me, he goes out onto the deck to soak in the hot tub before we get it on. What I think would be real exciting would be if you and I were getting it on in our room up there while he's soaking himself out on the deck."

I got the picture. This doll really was up to some nifty adventure. Fucking a young stud like me as a kind of hors d'oeuvres before taking on her regular lover. It would be like participating in a sexual extreme game. It made me kinda scared. And I really wanted to do it.

"What if he catches us?" I asked.

"That's where the adventure comes in," she said. "We have to be very alert while we're engaged in our coitus."

Jesus Christ! There it was. "Coitus." I guessed adults really *did* talk that way.

"Are you game?" she asked.

"Sounds like fun to me," I said. And at that point I really felt mature. It was a sexual challenge. And I'd accepted it.

She told me the address of The Eleutheria.

"Can you find that address?" she asked.

I assured her I could. I'd combed the Hills plenty in my Civic. I knew the street. I could find the address.

"Get there at six o'clock. No later. At six my guy will definitely be out on the deck and in the spa. Press the button on the callbox that's at the gate. When you get answered, say 'Carol 123.' That's the code I'll leave with the concierge. Madame Alexander will buzz the gate open. Drive in and pull into any empty stall you see. Park, then close the stall gate behind you so your car is hidden from view. Go to the front door. Ring three times. Madame Alexander will meet you at the door and lead you to the room I'll be in. Got it?"

I got it. And was I ever excited. I'd never even dreamed of being involved in a daring exploit like this. It was the most exciting game I'd ever even considered.

Carol had said I had the balls.

I'd show her that Tim Axelrod had the balls of a hero.

I actually strutted out of that dressing room.

I could hardly wait for the next day to come.

That next day I conned a little money out of my uncle. I wasn't sure what was coming up. But whatever it was, I didn't want to be caught without bread in my jeans.

That evening, I had no trouble finding The Eleutheria. Like I told you, I know the Hills. Give me an address there, I'll find it.

No problem getting in the gate. "Carol 123" did it. The car stalls with the masking gates? Cool!

Madame Alexander let me in. Is the Madame male or female? I wonder if anyone knows. His/Her uniform is unisex. So is the face and body. And who cares anyway?

The Madame led me right to the room Carol was in and without a word left me there.

Knock, knock.

Carol's voice called out. I would recognize that sultry voice anywhere.

"Come in, Tim."

She was wearing only a bra, panties, and gold stiletto shoes.

She opened her arms in welcome and I walked right up to her and gave her a hug and a deep kiss. Hot damn! Did I ever feel like a man of the world.

I asked the question.

"Is *he* here?"

"Right out there on the deck. In the spa. I've closed the outside door so he'll have to rattle it if he decides to come in before we're though doing what we're going to do. So, if we hear him coming, you've got to scoot into that closet there. Why don't you put your cloths in there now?"

I understood the deal. Loverboy wasn't supposed to come into the room. He was waiting for her out on the deck. But if he did come in, I needed to get into the closet where my clothes would be, without him seeing me. And Carol's job would be to get him back out onto the deck so I could make my

46

getaway.

That element of risk was a real turn-on.

"Would you like me to take your clothes off? Or would you rather do it yourself?" she asked.

I told her I wanted her to do it.

"That's what I prefer, too," she said.

She told me to take my shoes and socks off myself and put them in the walk-in closet. She would do the rest.

I'll tell you this. I *loved* having her undress me. As she did so, my eyes feasted on those bodacious boobs. I could hardly wait to get my hands on them.

When she got my shirt and undershirt off me, she ran her tongue around my nipples and sucked on them. Holy shit! Was that something else! Even my boner got a boner.

She sat on the edge of the bed, guiding me to stand facing her.

She took off my belt and unbuttoned the top button of my pants.

With my pants kinda loose around my middle, she tongued my bellybutton. Holy shit!! My bellybutton. While she was playing tongue games with my navel, her hands made caressing motions up and down my prick. It was still inside my pants and shorts, of course. But I felt it as if she was playing with my naked dick.

She had taken off my pants and briefs the day before. So I knew how that was going to feel. So I braced myself for it. I wanted it naturally. But I was worried, too. Last time she'd taken me in her mouth as soon as I was fully exposed. And I wanted her to do that again. But before, I'd had a preemie. I knew we mature men of the world weren't supposed to come at the drop of a hat. Or, in this case, on a suck from the lips. But the way I was throbbing already, I wasn't at all sure I could hold back.

But when she got my pants and skivvies off me, she didn't suck my cock. She ran her hands over my cock and balls, leaned around and encircled my nuts with her mouth, and swallowed them. Oops! I felt the pre-cum on my peckerhole. But no spurt. A relief. But at the same time, a kind of agony. My prick wanted to come. Nearly insisted on coming. But no preemie.

She gave a deep-throated lascivious chuckle.

"That's very good, Tim," she said. "You're doing just fine."

Nicest compliment I ever received.

She crawled up onto the bed. I followed her.

She faced away from me. She'd shed her high heels, but still had on her panties and bra.

I didn't have a clue what to do next. I just kinda lay there, facing her back. I wished I knew the moves in this situation. But didn't so I waited for her to give me some kinda directions.

"Spoon up next to me, Tim," she directed as she deftly removed her panties. "I want to feel that manly tool of yours against my skin."

That sounded like a good idea. I complied. I just hoped my "manly tool" would hold off coming all over her back. That would be *so* uncool.

My prick rested against Carol's ass-crack. Although my member throbbed, it felt like I was in control. At least for the moment.

"Wouldn't you like to caress my breasts?" she asked.

"Could you take off your bra?" I ventured.

"Later," she said. "For now, I would like the feel of your virile hands through my lacy bra."

If that's what she wanted, this definitely was not the time to argue. I reached around her and she guided my right hand onto her right boob. Shielded by bra or not, it was very exciting. My former feels at the girls I'd gotten to were more like furtive gropings. This was much more mature, and thus satisfying, to my mind. A man of the world does not insist on a lady removing her bra. I was getting the hang of sophistication.

"I'd like you in my vagina," she said in that husky, sexy voice.

She reached behind and gently took hold of my palpitating dong. I was so proud of myself. I hadn't come yet.

"Let me guide it in," she said.

She guided my dick down, but not as far forward as I thought the waiting cunt should be. She slipped me inside.

She was *much* tighter than I thought a snatch would be. But I was so horny I hardly gave a moment's thought to where "it" was as opposed to where it should be.

I pumped. Once, twice…good. That showed mature restraint. "Three times…" I couldn't hold back. "Four!" Oh-oh! Here I come!

As I pumped my essence into her there was a voice at the door.

"Karl! Are you coming out?"

Fuck almighty! I knew that voice. It was Uncle Mike's. And did he say "Carol" or "Karl"? What the Hell?!

"I'll be right out," was my companion's reply. Not the sultry voice I was used to. More of a masculine ring to it.

Carol hopped out of bed. And in that new voice she was using said, "That was great, Kid. I hope you got as big a kick out of it as I did."

She took off the brassiere. And guess what? The boobs stayed in the bra. They were falsies.

Carol turned towards me. Shit! She had a dong. And it was hard. To use another word, a phallus.

"Better get dressed and out of here before your uncle catches you, Tim," she said as she whipped off that blonde wig.

It was the vampire voice.

I had been cornholing a vampire.

And the vampire had just left the room, bare-assed and naked.

Was I ever pissed! I'd been betrayed. Here I thought I was losing my cherry to a babe. Instead I'd been fucking an actor in the ass.

But, wait a moment! Not only an actor. An actor who was my Uncle Mike's lover. *This* was the adult world? My uncle cheating on my aunt with a dude?

My rage gave way to confusion. I had to check this out.

Without putting my clothes back on, I peeked out onto the deck. The first thing I saw was two chicks, hand-in-hand, heading for either a pool or a spa. The moonlight on their bodies gave evidence that they were real women, not cross-dressers. And they were clearly a lot younger than the guy who had sucked my cock the day before and whom I had just cornholed.

The chicks giggled and slipped into the hot tub.

Over by the pool, lying on what appeared to be a mat or a mattress, were two guys. I didn't want to look too closely. I knew who they were. And who would want to see his uncle actually getting it on with another guy? Not me.

I wanted to get a better look at the two chicks in the spa. I slipped out of the room and into the shadows of an arbor.

Right in front of me I hear voices.. Female voices. At least two gals hiding in the shadows ahead of me. I strain to see if I can make out what they look like.

The two ladies were wearing masks. I could see that. And had capes on. Oh, no! Not more vampires. I'd had it with vampires.

They weren't aware of me behind them. I held very still.

"There he is, the rat," one of them said.

Christ Almighty! That voice! It was Aunt Olivia.

"Wait just a moment. Then we'll go out and surprise them."

It was another voice I recognized. Auntie Til's.

My head reeled. Two foxy chicks in the hot tub. My uncle and Karl

Tepes out in the moonlight nude and doing things I didn't want to know about. And Aunt Olivia and Auntie Til lurking in the shadows in masks and vampire cloaks. *This* was the adult world? I had stumbled onto a universe I couldn't process.

"Now!" Auntie Til said.

She and Aunt Olivia headed towards the pool. They interrupted whatever Uncle Mike and Karl (or Carol) were doing. The two men seemed to be urging the masked ladies to join them somehow. I crept closer, from behind one of the deck chairs to under a kind of sofa. I got close enough to overhear what was going on.

I saw Aunt Olivia and Auntie Til take off their masks. And it was pretty clear that Uncle Mike was very, very surprised at what he saw.

Then, Aunt Olivia was bawling Uncle Mike out. Then he told her she and Auntie Til were no better than he was.

Auntie Til said, "You know what, Olivia? He's right!"

Pretty soon my aunt and uncle were laughing. Would you believe it? Laughing.

Aunt Olivia was saying to him, "You know, Dear. I guess it's best to get this all out in the open. You like guys sometimes. I've found I like women. And we know we like each other."

Uncle Mike took her by the hand.

"Come on, Dear. I like what you're saying. Let's continue this discussion in private."

"My place or yours?" Aunt Olivia asked.

"Yours," he answered.

Off they went, arms around each other's waist, to what must have been the room Aunt Olivia and Auntie Til had been staying in.

That left Auntie Til and Karl alone with each other.

"Do you ever like to make love to women?" Auntie Til asked him.

"Not really," Karl said. "How about you? Do you dig guys?"

"Tried it once. Didn't like it," she answered.

Auntie Til went over to the spa.

"Hey, you two. Care for a threesome?" she asked.

"The more the merrier," one of the girls answered.

Auntie Til removed her cape and set her mask down by the side of the tub. She slipped into the tub with the chicks.

That left Karl all by himself.

I came out of hiding.

"I guess that leaves the two of us," I said to him. "Do you have any more tricks to show me?"

"Do I ever," he laughed.

Karl and I returned to his room. Where he taught me plenty.

* * *

That was three years ago, when I learned that Hollywood is AC/DC. I now know I can swing both ways. Here at Stanford I have about the same number of dates with dudes as with chicks. Which, as near as I can tell, gives me more action than the stupes who only know how to swing one way.

Confused about sex? Not me. Not since that evening and night at The Eleutheria. Hollywood had gone AC/DC. So did I.

PART TWO

EDUCATING
CHASTITY

EDUCATING CHASTITY

It was Saturday morning, and Jimmy thought he could sleep in late. But he did *not* sleep in. Sunshine was flooding into the bedroom through the open window. Jimmy was a fresh-air fiend, and whenever he was home, that window remained open to let in the bracing air.

It was seven o'clock and he had to get up to go to the bathroom.

He went, flushed, brushed his teeth, and flossed.

Still no sign of Barbie stirring.

When he got back to the kitchen, the water in the coffee maker was beginning to boil.

He was just getting a couple of coffee cups down from the cupboard when he heard the toilet flush. Time to go let Barbie know that coffee would be ready when she was.

Jimmy went to the bedroom and sat on the edge of the bed. The bathroom door was open and Jimmy could hear her brushing her teeth. He got up to look in the bathroom and saw her standing at the basin.

She rinsed her mouth and, looking in the mirror, saw him standing in the bedroom observing her.

"Jimmy!" she said. "Good morning."

"Yeah," was all he could muster. "I came to tell you I have some coffee brewing in the kitchen."

"To Hell with the coffee," she said. "I'm horny. And I'll just bet you are too."

"Don't you have to get ready to go to school?" he asked, not being able to think of anything else to say.

She looked at the clock on the dresser.

"We have plenty of time. I want to go back to bed. With you."

As she headed for the bed, Jimmy went to the open window to pull down the shade.

"Leave the shade up," she said. "We always do it in the dark. I want to see what we're doing."

Reluctantly, Jimmy abandoned the shade. Neither of them was exactly very experienced in lovemaking. Jimmy was nineteen, and had had furtive groping and clumsy sex with a couple of girls before Barbie. And currently he was having an affair with Chastity Hammerschmidt as well as with Barbie. But Barbie was the first girl he had taken to his bed. She was his "regular" and they had had sex off and on at his apartment for a couple of months now.

Barbie was eighteen, and was a virgin the first time Jimmy seduced her. He wasn't actually sure who had seduced whom. But he hoped he was the initiator.

He had met her when he was still going to San Diego City College the previous semester. They had necked in his car, and he had felt her up enough times. But he was somehow reluctant to get to 'third base' in the discomfort of his car.

And then, after a couple of months of necking and petting in the car, he had hesitatingly invited her up to his place for coffee. Nature had taken its course. He got her into bed and gave her a clumsy, inexperienced fucking. And now they were an 'item.'

As Jimmy was still dithering near the window, Barbie turned away from the bed and walked over to him.

As she approached him, her breasts jiggled delightfully. Jimmy had groped several breasts in his spotty amatory career. And he knew this was a fine pair.

Barbie kissed him on the soft part of his neck.

She completely surprised him by what she said next.

"You dirty young man," she said. "What you need is a shower."

"A shower?"

"You heard me. We've never taken a shower together. And I think it's high time. What do you think?"

"Yeah," Jimmy agreed. "I guess so."

She led the way into the bathroom.

She turned on the water in the shower, regulated the heat to a comfortable warmth, took his hand, and led him in.

All Jimmy's reluctance vanished. As a matter of fact, he nearly believed the shower idea had been his in the first place. At any rate, he fully endorsed the idea as if it *had* been at his instigation.

"Get your head into the water," he urged. She ducked her head into the needles of warm water. Jimmy shampooed her head.

While he was running his soapy hands through her hair, Barbie squeezed some shampoo into her hands, lathered them up, and began to shampoo his pubic hair. As his dick rose, she circled her hands around it and began to gently shampoo his balls.

She ducked her head under the shower to rinse the suds out of her hair as Jimmy rubbed one sudsy hand around her breasts as the other caressed her ass.

When they had helped each other get worked up close to a climax in the shower, Barbie had had enough.

"Maybe we'd better dry off and get into bed," she suggested.

"Yeah," he said. "Let's hop into the old sack."

Drying each other off with the one towel in Jimmy's bathroom maintained the sexual tension that had built up in the shower. But the couple was so anxious to get into bed and get involved in more feeling and fondling that neither was completely dry when they flopped down on the sheets.

The lovemaking that followed ran its soggy course.

Jimmy scooted down to where he could do something to her that the sex manual they read called cunnilingus. Jimmy's friend Vince told him it was called muff diving in the real world.

Barbie urged him to squirm around where she could get his phallus, her word for a dick with a hardon, into her mouth.

They then proceeded on to Position 69. But Jimmy didn't have that name for it yet.

After they'd both come, they lay in each other's arms in deep satisfaction.

When the post-coital lethargy began to wear off, Jimmy said, "The coffee's still waiting for us in the kitchen. And I have a box of Krispy Kreem donuts to go with them. How about some breakfast?"

"Jimmy's a dear," Barbie thought. "But he can't make coffee for shit. It's more like scared water than coffee." And the thought of donuts for breakfast was even more of a turn-off than his weak excuse for coffee. It was time to beg off again. She looked at the clock on the dresser.

"Gosh, Jimmy," she said. "Time certainly does go fast when you're having fun. Doesn't it? I've got to rush now if I'm going to get to class on time."

Actually, she had time to get to the student union at the school and get a decent cup of coffee and a Danish to go along with it well before class began.

"Yeah," Jimmy agreed. "I don't want to hold you up."

In truth, he was ready for her to go. He wasn't much for post-sex conversation.

"I'll just take myself another shower," she continued. "A quick one. All by myself. Then, I'll have to go rushing off."

In answer, Jimmy merely grunted and eased himself out of bed.

While Barbie showered, Jimmy slipped on yesterday's underwear and pants and went to the kitchen.

By the time he'd had two cups of coffee and two donuts, Barbie was standing next to him. She gave him a peck on the cheek. He didn't stand up, but just muttered, "So long. Have a nice class."

"I'll be back after class," Barbie said. "I've left my overnight bag in the bedroom."

"Yeah, fine," he responded.

And she was out the door.

Now that she was out of the place, Jimmy pondered the situation.

He and Barbie had met at City College before he dropped out of school from lack of interest and got himself a job at CIMCO. One thing led to another, and the two of them ended up 'going steady.'

It had been nice having a regular girlfriend. Neither one of them was awfully experienced in lovemaking when they first got together. But since he and Barbie had become an item, they'd been able to experiment a lot. Jimmy had bought a book, *Sex for Dummies,* and that had helped a lot. And they had recently become fairly comfortable with sex.

And now, he'd arrived at the hard part. He had to dump Barbie. Not an easy thing to do. He knew she'd make a scene of some kind. And he knew he'd really hate that.

He had another donut.

Well, there was no way of getting around it. His job at CIMCO seemed like a dead-end situation. And he could see only one way to get ahead in life. Marry Chastity Hammerschmidt. Now *there* was a great career move. Chastity was the only child of the CEO and owner of CIMCO, Mrs. Hammerschmidt, herself.

Chastity was a fine girl. But Jimmy was actually afraid of her mother, Mrs. Hammerschmidt. His boss was very attractive middle- aged woman. *Golly, she might even be as old as forty. Built like a brick shithouse, though.* With her as a mother-in-law, who could tell how high a guy could raise himself in the company? The young man had visions of truly being upwardly mobile.

But, first, he had to get rid of Barbie. She was in his way. The question was, how to do it in as painless a way as possible.

Well, his friend Vince would be coming by in about a half-hour. Vince was really experienced with chicks. He'd get advice from him.

So Jimmy put the box of donuts away, cleaned up the coffeepot a bit, and headed to the bathroom to shower away the accretions from the morning's exertions and get ready for Vince's visit.

Vince came by Jimmy's place most Saturday mornings. It was practically a ritual. They played a couple of games of Yahtzee, polished off a bottle of wine, nibbled some chips and dip, and gabbed. They talked about sports and women. Mostly women.

Jimmy provided the chips and dip. Never anything that required any preparation. He also was the one who had the Yahtzee dice and score cards. They played for a penny a point, just to keep it interesting. Vince brought the bottle.

Vince was Jimmy's friend. Truth to tell, his only friend. They had met in Mrs. Haddox's seventh grade homeroom back in middle school. Although different in nearly every way, the friendship clicked. Vince was muscular, bright, and handsome. Vince was still a good friend, even six years after they met. Jimmy now had a job.

Vince still attended night school at Mesa Community College, and enjoyed his classes very much. He particularly liked English Lit. But he was looking for a job. Jimmy was happy to have a job, and could not understand how anyone could like school. Especially English classes. Vince worked out regularly at a gym. Jimmy hated working out. Even the smell of a gym was unpleasant to him.

When Vince arrived at Jimmy's, they went to the kitchen. Jimmy got out the dip and chips. Vince uncorked the bottle of wine. They went into the living room with their refreshments. Jimmy had already set out the Yahtzee game.

As they played through the first set, Jimmy's mind was more on what he wanted to talk to Vince about than on the game. Vince threw a Yahtzee which made him the winner. So Jimmy owed him fifty-three cents. Jimmy was ahead of his friend, though, in the amount of wine and munchies he had consumed.

Jimmy paid Vince in accordance with the difference in their scores, poured himself another glass of wine, and settled back, showing he would rather gab than play a second round.

"So, Pal," Vince said, refilling the jelly glass they used as wine glasses at Jimmy's. "Looks like you have something on your mind. Spit it out."

He settled back in his chair to listen.

"It's about Barbie," Jimmy replied.

"Yeah, of course. You got woman problems of some kind, don't you?"

"You bet I do. I've got a big one."

"Go on."

"I've got to dump Barbie."

"Oh," Vince chuckled. "*That* kind of big problem. It's always messy."

"I'm hoping you can clue me in on how to get rid of her without hurting her feelings."

"Oh, I can tell you that," Vince said assuredly. "You can't."

"I *can't?*"

"No way. Getting into a heavy relationship is easy. Getting out if it is a pain in the ass."

"Thanks a lot."

"You're welcome."

"I know you've broken relationships with girlfriends yourself," Jimmy nudged his friend.

"Yep! Now it's your turn. Welcome to the club. You'll not only have to go through it a few times. You'll get dumped by a few dolls yourself. No matter whether you're the dumper or the dumpee, it stinks. But let me tell you something, Jimmy. As painful as it is, a sweet relationship is worth it. Now there are obviously loads of couples who hit it off so perfectly, they make it a permanent thing. And that's about as cool as it can get. But so far, for me, and most of the guys and gals I know, it hasn't happened yet. I don't want to get into a permanent arrangement, like marriage for instance, until I'm financially secure, and so head-over-heels stuck on the chick that I know I can make a lifelong commitment. Chicks feel even stronger about that, usually. They're the ones stuck with motherhood and all that shit. So that means breaking off a relationship, either by the guy or the gal, at some point before the perfect match is found. There's someone out there for me. And I'm here for her. And when the time comes, we'll click. Until then, it's a case of dump and get dumped."

"Always?" Jimmy wondered.

"No, not always. I've had a couple of times when it worked out that me and my girl saw the handwriting on the wall and called it quits without anyone feeling hurt. It's rare. And maybe that'll be your case. Tell me all about what's happening between you and Barbie. There's still plenty of wine in the bottle."

Jimmy unloaded his story on his pal.

"I met another girl, Vince. It all really began at the movie house. I went to see 'Ninja Werewolves' all by myself. Barbie wasn't interested in seeing it at all."

"Smart babe," Vince remarked.

"No comment. Well, I was sitting in the theater all by myself, with my popcorn and Pepsi, watching the movie. Not many people in the theater. It was a Sunday matinee, and the house was pretty empty.

"A gal came down the aisle and sat beside me. All I noticed was that it was a dame, but didn't pay too much attention.

"Pretty soon, her hand was on my thigh. I kind of gave a start and wondered what the Hell. Nothing like that had ever happened to me before."

"Me neither," Vince chuckled. "Not in a movie house anyway."

"Her hand kept moving up and down on my thigh. You know – like caressing it. I sat stock still. I didn't dare even move a muscle. For fear she would stop."

"Poor guy," Vince said in mock concern.

"I wondered if anyone else in the theater could see what was going on. I mean, in a way it was kind of embarrassing."

"Yeah," Vince said. "You should have told her you were a good boy, and that she should scram," was the good natured response.

"Shut up, you jerk. You want to hear this or not?"

"My lips are sealed."

"Go to Hell," Jimmy replied in a friendly way.

"Go on," Vince urged. "I'm all ears."

"Next thing you know, her hand was resting right on my fly. I like to come right then. I don't think I ever sprung such a boner before."

"Yeh, yeh, yeh" Vince encouraged. "Go on, Pal. Go on!"

"Well, she's fumbling around trying to unzip me. I just sat there frozen. She finally gets me unzipped and my peter came surging out of my pants."

"Yeah, and?"

"And I came right onto her hand and all over my fucking pants. What a mess."

"Yes, and what then?" Vince asked.

"This chick whispers, 'Meet me in the lobby.'"

"So, as you can imagine, I hurried up the aisle to meet her."

"Leaving the Ninja Werewolves behind," Vince kidded.

"I get to the lobby, embarrassed like. My pants all covered with cum. I felt like everyone would be looking at me and laughing."

"Forget the cum. Tell me about the chick," Vince urged.

"Yeah. I got to the lobby, and who do you suppose I find there waiting for me?"

"I'll bet I could guess. But I'd rather you told me."

"Chastity Hammerschmidt."

"Your boss's daughter."

"Exactly. She was smiling at me kind of funny like. Needless to say, I was flabbergasted. Blown out of my friggin' mind. Practically speechless.

"She said, 'Can we go to your place?' I asked her if she knew where it was. She did. So she went to her car and I went to mine. And we drove here.

"She got here first and was waiting outside by her car. It's a Beemer, late model coupe."

"Nice," Vince said.

"Yeah, nice all right. She's rich so I guess she can drive whatever she wants. That is, her mom's rich, so that means she's rich.

"We came up here. She was carrying a laptop computer with her. I didn't know why she'd want a laptop here, but I wasn't going to ask dumb questions at a time like that.

"We get up here, I ask her would she like a cup of coffee or something. She goes, 'Coffee'll be fine.' She puts the goddam computer on the sink counter and plops herself down on a chair. She looks at me with a smirk. I put some grounds in the Mr. Coffee, pour water in, and push the button.

"The coffeemaker was gurgling, and she was smiling at me real nice. I sit down at the table across from her.

"She goes, 'I guess I kind of gave you a surprise back there at the movie house, didn't I?'

"'Uh, yeah,' I said."

Chastity told Jimmy that her mother was very strict and moralistic. And she kept a tight rein on her daughter. But now that she had a car of her own, Chastity had the freedom to see more what life was about than before.

After graduating from a religiously based girls' high school in La Jolla, she was sent to Saint Hyacinth's Academy for Young Ladies, located in Encinitas.

At the Academy, Chastity learned all about how to be religious, and how to live up to her name. That is what she learned from the instructresses, those dour teachers dressed in depressing black. But she learned much more from the friend she made there named Dorabelle.

Dorabelle was a year older than Chastity, and much wiser to the ways of the world. And she opened Chastity's eyes to a whole new universe. It turned out that Chastity became a very enthusiastic student of an erotic universe she had not even guessed existed before.

Dorabelle, like all the girls in the college, had a laptop computer. And she had downloaded an ebook into her hard drive, a volume entitled *Dr. Morris' Marriage Manual*. Naturally, Chastity downloaded the work into her own laptop. And what a load of surprises lurked within those cyberpages. The two girls read the amazing material and discussed it very much in private. Dorabelle had a married sister who had additional information she had learned about the masculine sex. When Dorabelle put it all together for Chastity, both girls were delighted.

Chastity thought book learning was all very well. It provided grist for delightful fantasy after exciting fantasy. But she was quite aware that out there, in the "real world," the thrill of experiencing what the learned Dr. Morris described was what she *really* needed to explore.

Chastity came to the offices at CIMCO regularly to see her mother. And she looked over the young men working there. She screened each one in her mind to choose who would best suit her needs.

"And she chose me," Jimmy told his pal Vince.

"Good choice," Vince answered. "Did she say why?"

"She said she thought I was cute," Jimmy answered, half embarrassed, half bragging.

"Go on," Vince urged.

It was easy enough for Chastity to find out Jimmy's name. And the company records gave his address, birthday, and additional information she didn't need.

She began her own little surveillance system. When she had the time, she parked on his street and saw his comings and goings. She observed that he often brought a red-headed girl to his apartment.

"Meaning Barbie, of course," Vince interjected.

Jimmy agreed that it was Barbie that Chastity had seen coming there.

And staying there for extended periods of time.

That was exactly what Chastity needed to know. Jimmy was clearly a man of the world. He had a girlfriend, and he had sex with her. Precisely the right background. She didn't need a staid virgin to guide her into the pleasures described by Dr. Morris in his ebook.

So, on that Sunday afternoon, she had followed his car to the movie theater, waited until he'd bought his ticket and entered, and then followed. She had figured out from her reading how to capture his attention. And, golly! It had worked. Here she was in his kitchen, drinking his coffee, and telling him she wanted sex lessons.

Jimmy saw this as his big chance. Here was the boss's daughter, the only child of the Dragon Lady herself. The image burst upon his mind immediately. This young lady clearly was smitten by him. Bed her. Then wed her. Then it was reasonable to imagine he would be catapulted into upper management. And when the old lady died, hurray! Jimmy Kittelson. President of the company. CEO. Mr. Gotrocks. The trick was to play along with this chick's whims.

"Sex lessons, huh?" he'd said, trying to get a fix on what Chastity had in mind and how he could use that not only to get laid but to get her absolutely committed to him.

She told him about Dr. Morris' book that was downloaded into her laptop. She wanted to try out some of the amazing things the good doctor had written about.

"You mean, different ways of doing it?" Jimmy proffered.

"Yeah. Of course," she enthused. "Like I've written down some of the things, and I want you and me to do each of them. It's one thing to read the stuff. That gets me all hot and sexy feeling. But I don't think you really know what it's all about until you *do* it. What do *you* think?"

Jimmy could not agree more. After all, he never was much of a one for booklearning. Even though *Sex for Dummies* had actually taught him just about everything he knew.

"First," Chastity said, somewhat pedantically. "There are the body parts involved. I want to be sure I'm using the right name for the right parts. Okay?"

"Okay," Jimmy agreed, thinking this was a pretty lame way to go about getting laid. But it seemed like a start, anyway.

He told Vince how Chastity and he had talked about body parts.

She knew the Latin and medical names. Jimmy taught her the street names.

She had some index cards and dutifully wrote down the vernacular terms followed by the medical ones she knew from reading Dr. Morris' book: cunt, prick, clit, fuck, blow job, come, tits, hardon, twat, jism… The list filled five index cards.

"So now you had the vocabulary for the lessons," Vince smiled. "I guess that's a start. Sounds like a pretty cold way to get under way."

"Right," Jimmy agreed. "Next she gave me a list of the things she wanted to try. I knew some of the names, but not all of them. Hey, I've got the list around here someplace. Want to see it?"

Vince wanted to see the list, and Jimmy found it in a drawer.

"Here it is. Look it over. You probably already know all these."

Vince read the list, chuckling several times.

Not only did Vince know the names for the techniques and positions. He had taught the terms to his friend, glossing the terms used in *Sex for Dummies.*

Vince knew all the practices described in Doctor Morris' text. He had essayed many, but hardly all. There were several that he knew he would always shun.

"Wow, Dude," Vince exclaimed. "That is one Hell of a list. You mean this good looking babe wanted you to do all these things with her? You hit the jackpot, Chum."

"Do you know all those words?" Jimmy wondered.

"Don't you?" Vince asked.

"I do now, Jimmy boasted.

"Doctors," Vince scoffed.

"Doctors," Jimmy agreed with the tone of voice that showed disdain.

Chastity asked Jimmy if he had the time to get started on the lessons right then. Since Barbie wasn't coming over that Sunday afternoon, he was free to begin what he thought of as the courtship of Chastity Hammerschmidt.

They finished their coffee, and Jimmy escorted Chastity into his bedroom. She brought her laptop with her, set it up, and accessed her ebook.

"First, I guess we ought to take off our clothes," Chastity announced.

"Good idea," Jimmy agreed enthusiastically.

Chastity was absolutely matter-of-fact when taking off her clothes. Barbie was always provocative in doing so, which was much more arousing for Jimmy. But when he got a good look at Barbie's body, his physiology reacted. Chastity was actually somewhat more attractive than Barbie. Jimmy already knew Chastity would be no match for her mother's obvious charms, even clothed. Chastity was a very attractive young lady. Mrs. Hammerschmidt was va-va-voom! But from a different age, a different stratus, and with that dour, demanding CEO personality.

It was time to begin the first lesson.

"First, though," Jimmy said. "We should engage in foreplay. Just hopping right to it isn't as…"

"No," Chastity pouted. "I don't want to waste time on anything that isn't in the book. I can guess what foreplay is, but Dr. Morris doesn't deal with 'playing.' So, if you don't mind, let's get right down to the lessons."

Jimmy didn't feel like arguing. He would miss the foreplay. After all, he always found that 'getting there is half the fun.' But, if this chick just wanted to 'do it,' then, he would *do* it.

Chastity looked through her index cards, then checked out what Dr. Morris had to say.

"Let's start with 'blow job,'" she demanded. "Dr. Morris called it fellatio."

"Also known as 'cock sucking'" Jimmy said pedantically.

"That's very descriptive," she answered. "Actually, I don't really *blow* at all, do I?"

Jimmy didn't attempt to answer her because she had already gone down on him and was slurping away.

When she had finished, he merely told her it was good form to swallow the jism.

"It really tastes nice," she said agreeably. "How did I do?"

He told her she had done very nicely, but that next time she should fluff herself off while sucking his dick.

He had to explain that 'fluff off' for a female was like 'jacking off' for a dude.

"Oh, she said. "Like masturbation. I've already done that by myself. It'll be more fun to do it while giving you a blow job."

They had gone through lesson one. Now her tongue met his, and they played tongue tag. Which set off a new set of spasms through her body.

When she calmed down, and was breathing normally again, she said, "Thank you, Jimmy. That was nice."

"You're welcome, Chastity. Please feel free to come any time."

He wasn't sure she got the joke, because she didn't laugh or comment.

He continued relating the experience to Vince. He could tell from the tenting in Vince's pants that he was kind of getting off from Jimmy's tale.

Chastity asked Jimmy if she was no longer a virgin.

"Technically, you still are," he had to tell her. "In our next lesson we need to fuck. When I bust your cherry, then you'll no longer be a virgin."

Chastity had to make a note on a card – cherry = hymen.

She said she was happy since Dorabelle was still a virgin and she would beat her to getting to be a non-virgin. She asked what people called a non-virgin.

"A hot number," Jimmy told her. Chastity took a note.

She said she loved being a hot number, and indicated that she really wasn't quite ready to go on to the next lesson yet.

Jimmy told Vince, "I said that was fine by me. That I wasn't up to it right then myself. That it would take me a little while to recuperate."

Jimmy told Vince that he'd never thought he'd like being a teacher. But then, he'd never had considered giving a course in sex.

"No," Vince laughed. "I never ever thought of you as any kind of a student, much less a teacher."

Jimmy explained to Chastity that it was, indeed, time for recess. He told her she should go in and shower off while he cleaned things up.

He changed the sheets while she showered. Then he showered himself.

When they were showered and dressed, Jimmy said, "I'm famished, Chastity. I've got to get something to eat."

She was agreeable and they walked to the Chinese restaurant down the street and had some chop suey and tea.

"And that's the way Lesson One ended?" Vince asked.

"You better believe it," Jimmy answered. "She told me she was tired, and she wanted to go home."

"Then have you seen her since that first lesson?"

"Sure. We made a date for the next Sunday afternoon at my place. I cleared the decks, telling Barbie I had to go visit my mom. So, the next Sunday, Chastity came over, hot to trot. And we did the down and dirty."

"Meaning Lesson Number Two?"

"You bet your sweet biffy. Meaning Lesson Number Two.

"Chastity was ready and anxious to get her cherry busted. She was sick and tired of being a virgin and wanted to fuck.

"This time I told her that no matter what Dr. Morris had written that we needed to undress each other and do some foreplay to warm up to fucking. She didn't want to, but gave in.

"Actually, it turned out that she enjoyed undressing me and me undressing her. She liked me feeling her up and sucking her tits. She played some with my dong and gave it a few gentle sucks. I licked her snatch, and we were ready to get to fucking, missionary style."

The two friends had finished the bottle of wine Vince had brought over. Vince wanted to hear more. But Jimmy told him that was about all there was to tell about the 'lesson.' He'd deflowered the chick, she braced herself for it and didn't seem to feel much discomfort. The blood left on the sheet needed to get washed off before Barbie came back. But he could take care of that later.

He asked Vince if he'd like some coffee. No one ever really wanted some of Jimmy's coffee, so Vince suggested they go to an Irish style pub downtown where they went sometimes. They drove their separate cars down to Dinty's, ordered a Guinness each, found a table that suited them, and talked about sports rather than sex.

That next Sunday afternoon, Chastity arrived at Jimmy's, bright, bubbly, and enthusiastic to practice more of Dr. Morris' positions. And Jimmy was quite ready to re-assume his role as professor.

Chastity refused Jimmy's offer of a cup of coffee and a Krispy Kreem donut, claiming she could hardly wait to get started on the day's lessons. She led him into the bedroom, set up her laptop, and read off to him the four positions she had studied in preparation for class. Jimmy wasn't exactly sure of any of them, particularly the ones with the foreign sounding names.

They chose the one Dr. Morris called 'rear entry.' Jimmy told her everyone really called it 'doggy style.'

She laughed and wrote down a note on it.

In their foreplay, Jimmy played around a lot with her ass. She liked that.

He got her in a standard kneeling doggy position on the bed, rubbed some KY jelly on his prick, and slid it in.

In the course of the lesson, Jimmy became overly enthusiastic. And as a result of his exuberance, he caused Chastity's head to crash into the headboard. She started to cry.

Jimmy's reaction of placing her head on his shoulder was spontaneous and right. His apologies were merely annoying.

"Is there anything I can do for you?" he inquired when her sobs quieted down.

"Yes, Jimmy. Get me a couple of aspirin. My head hurts."

"Sorry, Chastity. I don't have any aspirin in the place."

"Tylenol then?" she asked hopefully.

"Nope. No pain killers at all. Would you like a cup of coffee?"

Chastity definitely did *not* want a cup of Jimmy's coffee.

She asked, "How about a Coke?"

"No Coke."

"Pepsi?"

"Uh-uh."

"Let's get dressed, Jimmy," Chastity said, a couple of loveable tears clinging to her pretty cheeks. "I want some aspirin. And I want a Coke. And I want to go out and get some air."

So, once dressed, and in a somber mood, the couple went outside to Jimmy's car. He pulled over to the curb outside a nearby drugstore, bought a tin of aspirin, then drove on to a McDonald's a few blocks beyond.

Seated at a booth at the McDonalds, each with a giant Coca-Cola, Chastity downed a couple of aspirin, sipped her drink through a straw, and felt her good nature returning.

She laughed.

"When you think about it, that was kind of funny, wasn't it?" Chastity bubbled.

Jimmy really didn't think so, and decided he needed a couple of aspirin himself. And he knew there was no medicine in the world that could assuage the embarrassment and ego-shattering hurt to his fragile male ego.

"I really messed up on that one," he told his friend.

"A royal screw-up, all right," Vince had to agree.

Bouncing your date's head off a headboard was something Vince could not comfort Jimmy about. Jimmy had been, indeed, a total klutz that time.

Jimmy was anxious to get on with his story to Vince. Because things *did* improve as the afternoon progressed.

"Do you want to go back to my place?" Jimmy asked Chastity, hopefully.

"Yes, Jimmy," Chastity replied. "I'm feeling better now. But just one thing."

"Yeah, what?"

"Stop somewhere and get a six-pack of Coke to keep in your refrig. For me."

Jimmy stopped on the way home at a Seven-Eleven and bought the beverage Chastity clearly enjoyed.

When they got back to his place, Chastity was over her headache and ready for the next three positions she had counted on learning that afternoon.

When they had run the course, the couple were both breathing hard.

"Goodness," Chastity said after she gained back her breath. "If Miss Carney could only have seen that!"

"Who's Miss Carney?"

"My gym teacher. She's always saying that it's blessed to stay in good shape. I guess she's right."

Jimmy agreed that Miss Carney really had something there.

Jimmy and Chastity showered, separately, went back to bed, and fell into naps.

"And that was all for that day?" Vince asked, disappointed that there might not be more.

"That was it for the day," Jimmy confirmed. "After our naps, we were too damned tired for anything else. I took her back to McDonald's where we each had a Big Mac, fries, and sodas. We agreed to meet the next week. I took her back to her car. And it was 'Hasta la vista, Baby.'"

Jimmy had come to a natural stopping place in his story. And the friends had finished drinking their stouts. So they paid the tab, went back to Jimmy's place, and Jimmy continued his story.

As soon as they settled down, Vince was eager to hear the rest of the story.

"So Chastity actually did come back the next Sunday?" Vince asked.

"Sure. She still had seven positions she wanted to try. I knew I was going to put the kibosh on some of them. Diplomatically, of course. After all, she *is* my ticket to the good life. I have to get her to marry me. But she has to learn there are some things that are just off-limits. There's no fucking way I'm going to run my tongue up her asshole. Or let her do that to me. And as to having her run her finger up my ass either. And as for those 'golden showers' No way!"

Vince agreed that there are some practices that are simply too repugnant to even consider.

Jimmy went on to tell his pal about the session he'd had with Chastity the previous Sunday.

When Chastity arrived punctually for her lessons, Jimmy had already brewed some coffee. They sat at the kitchen table, and while he sipped his coffee, Chastity drank a Coke.

As they enjoyed their beverages, Chastity showed Jimmy the list she had prepared for the day

"I know we can't get all of these in this afternoon," she told him. "Let's just see how far we get."

"There's no rush," Jimmy answered. "We'll go through the list, leaving out some of the stuff no *real* man does. And then, we'll go back and fine-tune the ones you really like."

They dutifully marched into the bedroom. Chastity set down her purse and booted up her computer

Jimmy didn't have a clue what the two positions with the foreign names were. And had only a hazy idea about the ones with the numbers. And a couple of them were not really clear in his mind.

"I guess I'd like to review what Dr. Morris has to say on some of these, Babe," he said.

When Jimmy was telling Vince about each one of Doctor Martin's positions he and Chastity had tried, his friend started to chuckle.

"What's so damned funny?" Jimmy asked.

"That little gal of yours is starting to get ahead of you, Jimmy. It sounds like she's one saucy piece."

Jimmy agreed and went on with his story.

He told his friend about the positions he and Chastity had engaged in.

When the session was over, Chastity seemed as satisfied as Jimmy, and settled into his arms. Their heartbeats were intense, and added to the intimacy of the moment. For the first time since the first 'lesson' there was more than a clinical feeling to what they were doing. Chastity had fond feelings for her 'teacher.' And for Jimmy, she had become more than a sex object and a ticket to the big time.

They lingered in each other's arms well past the time when their hearts had quieted down. They were enveloped in a kind of lovers' haze.

The couple showered separately. Enough, after all, was enough.

After showering and getting clothed, Jimmy asked Chastity if she would like something to eat.

Jimmy suggested going out to his favorite restaurant for some post-sex nourishment.

"McDonald's?" Chastity guessed.

"McDonald's," Jimmy said, with anticipation of a Big Mac gleaming in his eyes.

Chastity was not as big a fan of McDonald's as Jimmy was. She suggested Starbucks.

Jimmy told Vince, "I don't get it. A coffee house. I could have made us some coffee right here."

"But I'll bet you didn't have any pastries here, did you?"

"You're right, Vince. Pastries. That's probably why she wanted to go to Starbucks. And, besides, when we got there, she ordered a latte to go with a blueberry muffin. I don't know how to make a latte."

Over coffee and pastries, Chastity and Jimmy kept looking at each other and smiling. They held hands. No one watching would ever have taken them for student and teacher.

They returned to Jimmy's place, but they really had more need for sleep than for additional fucking, sucking, and fondling.

They napped, contentedly, in each other's arms, for about a half-hour. Jimmy awoke first, got out of bed, donned his bathrobe, and went into the front room.

He brewed a pot of coffee, took a cup of it to the living room, extracted a CD from his tower, and sat contentedly on the couch thinking of the young lady who had not only brought him so much pleasure in pursuit of her sex lessons but who, he felt sure, would be his angel who would carry him out of his lower middle-class world up into the world of privilege, prestige, and real class. He felt he deserved no less.

He closed his eyes, listening to Aimee Mann's album, *The Forgotten Arm.* As he was listening to "She Really Wants You," Chastity came tiptoeing through the room wearing one of Jimmy's t-shirts she had found in his dresser drawers. With his eyes closed, and being absorbed in the music, Jimmy didn't notice her. She sneaked into the kitchen, poured herself a Coke, and brought it into the living room, and quietly snuggled up next to him.

He wasn't startled by her. Keeping his eyes closed, he put his arm around her and held her close. He gently played with her tits and she kept him hard with her hand. Each felt strangely contented.

From time to time, one or the other would open his/her eyes long enough to reach for the beverage on the coffee table in front of them, take a sip, and then return to the closed-eyed fondling, absorbed in each other and the music.

When the song came to an end, Chastity said, "It's beginning to get a little late, Jimmy. But before I have to go home, I'll bet we can work in the next two lessons."

Jimmy was certainly game for two more 'lessons,' and led her back to the bedroom. He took off his bathrobe. She removed the t-shirt, and they studied the computer screen together to fathom the secrets of the next two moves described in the book.

Chastity was turned off by one of them, and Jimmy wanted to try it. It was the sixty-nine that they had skipped before because it sounded too complicated. They got into an argument about the matter.

Chastity got very angry, got dressed, and left the apartment in a huff.

"Bummer," Vince said, trying to keep from laughing. But he couldn't suppress his mirth, and burst out with guffaws.

"Knock it off!" Jimmy exploded. "It wasn't funny."

"No," Vince answered, but with merriment in his voice. "It's *not* funny, Jimmy. But it's not tragic either. When she thinks it over, she'll realize it wasn't your fault. And she'll be back. Once she thinks over the mechanics, no gal can resist trying sixty-nine."

"You think so?" Jimmy asked hopefully.

"Trust me," Vince told him.

Just then the telephone rang.

"I'll bet that's her now," Vince said.

"Gee! I hope so," Jimmy said, heading for the telephone.

"Hello."

"Hello. May I speak to Mr. James Kittelson?"

It was a female voice. A mature female voice. *What the Hell?*

"Uh…I'm Jimmy Kittelson."

"Fine, James. This is Mrs. Hammerschmidt."

Jimmy panicked. Mrs. Hammerschmidt. Chastity's mother. *And*, his boss lady. There could be Hell to pay. Was the old lady on the warpath? Was she calling to fire him for disturbing, or worse, fucking her daughter? Jimmy could barely blurt out an answer.

"Uh…Yes, Ma'am."

"I'm happy to hear you are at home."

"Me, too.."

"I need to see you, right away," the lady said. "Obviously I have your address. I'll be there in about fifteen minutes."

Jimmy was saying 'Fine" into the phone. But the buzz he heard informed him that Mrs. Hammerschmidt had already hung up.

Panic!

"Vince. You know who that was?"

"From the way you talked to whoever it was, and from the way you look, I'd guess it was probably the Angel of Death. And that she called to tell you she's coming to haul your ass off to Hell."

"Worse, Vince. Much worse. It was Mrs. Hammerschmidt."

"Chastity's mother?!"

"*And* my boss."

"What the Hell did she call about? And why are you so rattled?"

"She's coming here, Vince. In about fifteen minutes."

"Coming here? Why?"

"How the Hell should I know?" Jimmy panicked. "She didn't say. To fire me? To cut off my balls for diddling her daughter? How should I know?"

"Sure sounds like trouble."

"Trouble, Buddy? You want to hear 'trouble?' Barbie's class should be letting out about now. If she comes barging in here while the old lady is on my case, my goose will be cooked. You've got to help me."

"Anything, Old Pal," Vince assured him. "You know it's old Vince to the rescue. What do you want me to do? Go get a gun and shoot the old bag who's your boss out in the hallway? Get a couple of goons to abduct her to Timbuktu? What?"

"Haul yourself out of here and intercept Barbie," Jimmy pleaded. "She'll be getting off the bus down on Laurel Street. Don't let her come in on me while Mrs. Hammerschmidt is here."

"Oh," Vince said, relieved. "Can do. I'll go right now and hang out at the bus stop. Trust me. I can come up with some story that'll keep her away for…how long? An hour?"

"An hour should do it. But why don't you phone me in an hour and ask if the coast is clear. If not…"

"If not, I'll keep the little lady busy somehow until you're ready for her to return. Don't worry. I'm out of here like a flash."

Even as he was saying it, Vince was heading for the door, and was out of the apartment.

Jimmy was, of course, very nervous. He had to go take a piss something awful. He went to the bathroom, relieved himself, combed his hair, and sprayed some of his Old Spice over his body to make himself presentable.

Then, he went to the kitchen and brewed some coffee for the visitation as a good host should.

He was just beginning to pull himself together when the doorbell rang.

Oh my God! She's here.

Panic.

Jimmy opened the door and found his boss, and the mother of the young lady he'd been educating, standing there in a regal posture. He stood stock still and stared.

"Well, James. Are you going to just stand there gaping? Or are you going to invite me in?"

"Uh…Come in, Mrs. Hammerschmidt."

Mrs. Hammerschmidt was a very impressive looking woman. She was as beautiful as her daughter, or perhaps more so. At thirty-eight, her figure was maturely outstanding. She was dressed very stylishly, a fact wasted on Jimmy. At the office, he had been struck by her attractiveness, in a rather abstract way. As she entered his apartment, he was aware that her ass and her legs were enough to turn on…well…an older man.

"Coffee, Ma'am?"

"Suppose we sit down," Mrs. Hammerschmidt said in a way that seemed more an order than a suggestion.

"Yeah," Jimmy stammered. "Have a seat."

Mrs. Hammerschmidt sat on the sofa and patted the spot next to her.

"Why don't you sit here?" she ordered rather than suggested.

Jimmy sat next to the lady, quite stiff and upright.

"Do you know why I'm here?" she asked.

To give me Hell for fucking your daughter? To fire me for some kind of incompetence at work?

Neither answer seemed quite appropriate.

"No, Ma'am," Jimmy decided to reply. "I don't."

There. That was better than either of the answers that had first popped into his head.

"Are you quite sure that none of the other young men at the office have mentioned my visits to them?" the lady asked.

"No, Ma'am. I mean yes, Ma'am. No one's said anything like that."

"Don't lie to me, James. I will know if you are lying."

"Honest, Mrs. Hammerschmidt."

"That's good. Because I've told each one of them that if they so much as hint that I have visited them, I will not only fire them. I will see to it that no one will *ever* hire them. Ever! Do you understand?"

"Uh…I guess so."

"What I'm telling you, James, is that if you ever so much as breathe to another soul – anyone – that I came to your home here to see you, you will have cause to regret it to your dying day. Do I make myself clear?"

"Uh…Yeah. Clear."

Jimmy was confused by the direction the conversation was taking. Why must no one ever know about the visit? Why? Not a clue. He was uncomfortable that he had already told his friend Vince that the lady was coming. That, apparently, was a mistake. But he could swear Vince to secrecy. After all, they were pals. Weren't they?

"What I want you to know, young man, is that I came here to check you out."

Check me out? What the Hell does that mean? Keep mum and let her keep the floor.

"I have a daughter, Chastity. My only child," Mrs. Hammerschmidt went on.

Cripes! Here it comes.

"I intend for her to marry one of the young men who work at CIMCO. I will, of course, choose the man she marries. Someone who will be pleasing to her. But, more importantly, one who will please me when he becomes a member of my family. The one I choose will have made a great career move."

My very thoughts. My ticket to the top. She's come to tell me I'm the one for Chastity. And she doesn't even realize that Chastity has already…uh…

"I have checked out all your workmates. I call them our pack of stud muffins."

Stud muffins? Jesus!

"I hired you because I thought you might have the makings of being *the* very stud muffin who meets my qualifications. So you may consider this an interview for a possible promotion. But, let me emphasize again. All the other young men you work with have been interviewed. All are sworn to secrecy. And from the pool of candidates, I will choose the young man who pleases me most. And, I assure you, Chastity will marry the one I choose."

A competition with the other guys at work. Who would have guessed?

"Now we will begin with a few questions. They may not seem pertinent to you. Rest assured that every question, and everything we do here this afternoon, has meaning to me. And to your possible future. Are you prepared to answer me truthfully?"

"Yes, Ma'am."

"I'll know if you're lying. I'm like a living polygraph machine. One lie and it's over for you. Do you understand?"

Jimmy understood, and suddenly felt very intimidated. Was she going to ask whether he had nailed her daughter? Did she already know? He hoped she couldn't see his knees trembling.

"Very well, James. To begin with. Do you still have nocturnal emissions?"

Nocturnal emissions? What the Hell?

He was slow in answering.

"Nocturnal emissions, James. Wet dreams."

"Yes, Ma'am."

"Good. At your age that shows a healthy libido."

I guess that was the right answer.

"Do you masturbate?"

Yikes! What kind of question is that?

Jimmy was thrown by the question and hesitated.

"You know the word, don't you James?"

"Y…y…y..yes, Ma'am. I do."

"An honest answer, James. If you had answered otherwise, I would have known you were lying to me. A young man your age who still has wet dreams is also sure to be masturbating a great deal. Even if he is having sexual relations with the young ladies."

I guess she really doesn't know about me and Chastity. That's a relief.

"The answer clearly is yes. As you see, I am quite frank and forthcoming with you. You must continue to be as frank with me. You *do* see, don't you?"

"Yes, Ma'am."

"Now, tell me. Are you circumcised?"

Again he was thrown by the question, although it actually was no more personal than her previous ones.

"Circumcised, James. You know. Are you cut or uncut?"

"Cut, Ma'am."

Mrs. Hammerschmidt frowned.

"Oh, circumcised. Pity. It's a shame to be mutilated. But it's hardly your fault, is it?"

"No, Ma'am," he answered.

"Do you wear jockey shorts or the boxer kind?"

"Boxer shorts, Ma'am."

"Hmmm. Boxer shorts. That is healthier than the jockey kind. Very good.

"Take off your shoes and your belt, James," she ordered.

My belt? Jesus Christ, what is this?

He knocked off his shoes, stood up, and took off his belt.

"Now drop your trousers," she demanded.

Bewildered, he did so.

"Now show me your penis."

He felt quite intimidated. What kind of thing was that for a boss to ask of an employee. Oh, well.

He popped his prick out of the boxer's fly.

"You were honest about being circumcised."

Why would I lie about something like that?

She scrutinized his dick.

"Rather small," she said. "Yet an adequate size, I suppose. It's difficult to really tell though unless it's engorged. I won't ask you to get an erection, though, at the moment. I wouldn't want to embarrass you."

He stood there in a daze.

"Don't just stand there, young man, looking stupid. You may withdraw that thing back into your shorts."

It didn't take him a second to pull it back into the safety of his shorts.

Did I flunk on that one?

"Take off your shirt, James."

Jimmy was confused. Take off his *shirt?*

Jimmy came up with an inspiration to get his boss-lady off in another direction.

"Are you sure you wouldn't like a cup of coffee, Mrs. Hammerschmidt? I have some brewed in the kitchen."

"Take off your shirt," she ordered.

Shit. She sounds like a fucking drill sergeant.

"Yes, Ma'am."

"Your t-shirt as well. I want to see your torso."

Jesus Christ! My torso?

Off came the shirt and t-shirt. Jimmy draped them over a nearby chair.

"What a dreadful smell!" the lady exclaimed.

"What?"

"That smell when you take off your shirt. Do you use some kind of cheap cologne?"

"Old Spice, Ma'am."

"Old Spice," she exclaimed with distaste. "Are you attempting to hide some foul body odor?"

"No, Ma'am. Sorry if you don't like the smell."

"A man's natural smell, the musky odor from his armpits. That's what a man should smell like. Not 'Old Spice.'"

"Yes, Ma'am."

Jimmy was sorry he'd sprayed so much of the damned stuff on. The lady wanted to smell his armpit odor.

"Turn around and let me get a look at you."

Jimmy turned around, very uncomfortable at having his upper physique looked at critically. He wished he'd gone to the gym regularly. Like Vince. His own muscles were, he knew, nothing particular to brag about.

"You're a little puny, aren't you? Hard to tell when a man's fully dressed. I've seen worse though."

"Hmm!" Mrs. Hammerschmidt criticized. "Nothing that a bit of time at a gym couldn't remedy, though. Have you ever considered enrolling at a gym? One with all that Nautilus equipment? A healthy young muffin like you should consider it. It could work wonders."

"Oh, yes, Ma'am," Jimmy lied. "I was just saying to a friend of mine that I planned to sign up at this gym he goes to. We plan to work out together."

"Splendid. Kind of inspire each other a bit, eh? Competition in body building is probably a good thing. That's good thinking, James.

"You may put your shirt back on now," she smiled.

He hastily put on his garb.

Well, that one went pretty good. My case may not be hopeless yet.

"I assume that, like the other young men in CIMCO, you would not turn down the chance to marry my daughter."

"Oh, no, Ma'am. I would feel it a great honor to marry your daughter."

She then winked at him and said, "Now let's see how you are on technique. Where you are deficient, I will attempt to see if you are teachable."

Mrs. Hammerschmidt rose and very efficiently removed every stitch of clothing she had on. Jimmy wondered if it would be considered rude to stare at her during the process. But rude or not, he couldn't help but stare, fascinated.

"Now, for this part of our interview, we'll concentrate on that all-important matter of technique. And we should start with the soft kiss."

"Soft kiss?"

"Yes. We simply lick each other's lips. No sucking on the mouth. And certainly no tongue intrusion. Here. Let me show you."

She licked his lips, which he found to be quite exciting.

"Now, you try to do the same to me."

"Yes Ma'am."

Jimmy licked her lips.

"No, no, no, James. You *must* be more attentive. The middle of the lips get minimal attention. It is the edges that are the erogenous zones. Let me show you again."

When Mrs. Hammerschmidt licked his lips this time, Jimmy became aware that the edges of the lips really are where the 'erogenous zones' were. He wasn't sure he knew exactly what 'erogenous' was. He decided he had to add the word to his vocabulary.

He gave the lady a return soft kiss, which she declared "quite satisfactory." He wondered where all this was leading. But he was decidedly more comfortable with the situation as time went on.

"I think you will become quite accomplished with the soft kiss, James. It is very important as a beginning to romance.

"Now to proceed. Most women are intrigued by the vampire."

Yikes! I'm game for a lot. But if she's into sucking blood, I'm just going to have to bail.

"Here, James. Let me show you."

And before he could demure, she was biting him very gently on his neck. Really nibbling rather than biting. It was a pleasantly eerie feeling which caused tingling to run up and down his spine and into his balls. As strange as it was, it was a definite turn-on.

Now she teased playfully, for the first time in this interview.

"There. Now *you* are a vampire, too. Bite me back."

Jimmy did bite the lady's neck. But in his inexperience, he bit too hard, causing pain.

"Ouch! Too hard, James. I'm afraid you don't have the makings of a Count Dracula. We'll go on to something else."

With the kissing behind them, Jimmy's previous feelings of being intimidated morphed into confidence and even pleasure.

"What do you know of the *ars amatoria*?" the lady asked him.

That sounded like a dirty word he had never heard before. Jimmy could not answer. He simply looked dumbfounded.

"Ars amatoria," Mrs. H. repeated. "The art of love."

"Oh, that," Jimmy answered, relieved. "I guess I know quite a bit."

"Have you, by any chance, read Doctor Morris' book on the subject?"

Now Jimmy felt himself on firm ground. He couldn't tell her how he had come into possession of Doctor Morris' ars amatoria. But he could show off to the lady that he really did know a thing or two.

Jimmy recited the names of some of the positions he had learned about in the good doctor's book.

Mrs. Hammerschmidt ordered him to disrobe again and to demonstrate a few positions.

Jimmy complied readily.

"I guess so, Mrs. Hammerschmidt."

James and his boss did number sixty-nine and rear entry in what he thought was a satisfactory manner.

Neither Mrs. Hammerschmidt nor Jimmy was aware that there were two observers of the passionate scene unfolding on the sofa. A man and a woman, totally nude, were standing in the doorway that led from the livingroom to the bedroom.

"Now, we will both get our clothes back on, and then we can finish the interview," Mrs. Hammerschmidt declared.

Jimmy was pleased to discover that the knowledge he had gained from Chastity's laptop had served him well.

There was no discussion as they dressed. There really did not seem to be anything to say.

When they were dressed, Mrs. Hammerschmidt sat down on the sofa.

"Come sit beside me, James. I just have two more questions for you. Then I'll be off and about my business."

"Yes, Ma'am."

"As far as your records show, you are what I would call 'under educated.' Do you have any plans for future education?"

"Oh, yes, Mrs. Hammerschmidt," Jimmy lied. "I was going to get the papers ready this very afternoon to re-enroll in City College. I miss the classes a lot. What subjects would you suggest?"

"A young man cannot be too conversant with the classics of literature. Had you thought of majoring in English Literature?"

"My very favorite subject," he lied through his teeth. If there was any subject Jimmy detested, it was English.

"Wonderful," the lady said. "And those plans of enrolling at a gymnasium. I hope you are sincere about that."

"Oh, absolutely, Ma'am."

Physical exertion at a smelly gym was about as close to the pits in Jimmy's plans as courses in English literature. But, to be upwardly mobile…

"That's just grand, James. Now, I'll be on my way. I'll be interested in hearing about your intellectual and physical education as time goes on."

Both were still seated on the sofa when the two people who had previously intruded, unobserved on the 'interview' on the sofa, entered.

Barbie spoke first.

"Well, Jimmy. Fancy meeting *you* here. I see you've been entertaining company."

Vince chimed in behind her.

"I really tried to keep Barbie out, Chum. But she wouldn't be restrained."

Jimmy gaped.

"How the Hell did *you* get here?" he asked the intruders.

Mrs. Hammerschmidt stood.

"Perhaps you would care to introduce me to your friends, James."

Jimmy's query, "What are you two doing here," was actually a very good question. And one he never did get a full answer to.

Here is a description of what had actually transpired.

When Mrs. Hammerschmidt had telephoned Jimmy, somewhat less than an hour previously, Vince was sent off to forestall Barbie's intrusion on the meeting between Jimmy and his boss lady. As requested by his friend, Vince had walked down to the bus stop, and was standing there when Barbie got off the bus.

"Gee! Hi, Vince. What are *you* doing here? Catching a bus?"

"Hi ya', Barbie. No. I'm not here to catch a bus. I came here to meet you."

"Meet me? Golly. What's up? Has something happened to Jimmy?"

"Naw. Jimmy's okay. I just wanted to chat with you. Why don't we go somewhere and get something to drink?"

"What's this all about, Vince?" Barbie asked, suspicious. "We can go up to Jimmy's apartment and have something to drink and we can chat there."

The fact was that Vince had not really thought through a stratagem to keep Barbie at bay from the apartment. And he felt quite clumsy at this point.

"No. Not a good idea. You see, Jimmy's kind of busy right now."

"Busy?" She was perplexed and even more suspicious than before. "What's he busy doing?"

"His boss called and is there talking to him. He doesn't want to be disturbed."

"His *boss* is there? That old lady he works for? Why is she at his place? Why can't she talk to him at work?"

"I don't know," Vince admitted. "Jimmy thinks she's considering him for a promotion. Maybe she wants to check out his apartment. See if he's neat and tidy and all that. You can tell a lot about people by how they maintain their living quarters"

Barbie wasn't quite convinced, but thought perhaps there might be a tiny chance that Vince was right.

"I don't know," she said. "I don't have any idea about how businesses work. But that sounds a little bit weird to me."

Vince latched onto Barbie's near acceptance of his story. And, he thought it might be correct. It seemed unlikely that the boss knew Jimmy was involved with her daughter. The more likely reason for her visit was the one he had just made up. He would stick with that story and try to convince Barbie that it was true.

"So you see, Barbie. This meeting with his boss could be very important for Jimmy's future. She will see that he keeps his apartment in pretty good condition for a bachelor. And he'll probably get that promotion. But if you should go barging in there, that could disrupt everything. Jimmy doesn't need any distraction while he's trying to impress the boss, does he?"

"Hmm," Barbie wondered. "You may be right, Vince. I don't want to mess up Jimmy's chances of getting a promotion."

"Exactly!" Vince agreed. "So let's us go somewhere, sit out some time, and in about an hour I'll give Jimmy a telephone call and see if the old lady's left yet."

"No," Barbie said. "I have an even better idea."

"Yeah? What?"

Vince was a bit disturbed about what the "better idea" might be.

"I can sneak into Jimmy's apartment by the back way," Barbie explained. "You know that bedroom window he always leaves open when he's home because he's such a fresh air fiend? I'm going in that way and take a peek into the livingroom to see if they're there instead of in the kitchen. Then I'll sneak out again."

"Bad idea," Vince said. "The old lady might just go into the bedroom to see if Jimmy keeps it neat. If she catches you in there, what's she going to think? It could blow the whole deal for Jimmy. No, we'd better go somewhere else until she's left."

"No, Vince!" Barbie insisted. "I can look in the bedroom window. If the old lady's not there, I can enter without her being wise to it. I can peek into the livingroom, see how it's going for Jimmy, and be out in a jiffy. I'm going!"

There was so much determination in Barbie's voice that Vince knew he couldn't stop her.

"I think it's a rotten idea," he said. "But, if you're going, I'm coming with you. I can help you in and out the window. You might need me."

"That would be a great help, Vince," Barbie agreed. "I appreciate it. Come on. Let's go."

And go they did.

The two made their way to the back of the apartment complex and climbed the stairs very stealthily. When they got to the bedroom window, they both peeked in. The room was empty. So far so good.

The window was wide open, the way Jimmy always liked to keep it. Vince entered first, very, very quietly. He reached outside and lifted Barbie in effortlessly. As he was lifting her, Barbie was acutely aware of his musculature. Aware, as a consequence, that he was a well-built stud. Somehow, she hadn't really taken in that fact quite so forcefully before. After all, he had never previously lifted her. It was a pleasant sensation.

They could hear a woman's voice in the next room. The boss lady was there. Jimmy had told Barbie about the "Dragon Lady." This was a chance to see the old witch.

They tiptoed to the livingroom door. They made not a sound. Not a peep.

The door was ajar. Barbie scooted down so Vince could glance above her. Four inquisitive eyes peeked into the livingroom.

And what did they see?

A very attractive naked lady was sitting on the couch.

That's the 'Dragon Lady'? The 'old witch'? Jimmy's description of his boss lady hardly does her justice. She's gorgeous.

And Jimmy was standing in front of her, bare-ass naked.

What kind of business is going on in there?

All Vince could think of was "Oh-oh!"

84

They could hear what the two people were saying.

"Oh, no, Ma'am," Jimmy was saying. "I would feel it a great honor to marry your daughter."

Marry her daughter? That rat!

"This will put us on a more even playing field," the boss-lady was saying.

Barbie had had enough.

She tiptoed to the bed, dragging Vince behind her by the hand.

She whispered in his ear.

"Vince, I'm so angry!"

"I understand."

"I'm going to get my revenge on that rat," Barbie vowed.

Vince heard himself whispering back, "I can't blame you."

He was surprised, and more than a little pleased, when she took off her blouse. She was not wearing a bra.

Well, Jimmy is my friend. And I'd do nearly anything for him. But he also is kind of a rat. Two-timing this babe. She deserves to revenge herself on him.

Barbie sat provocatively on the side of the bed and patted the spot next to her in what could only be construed as an invitation for Vince to sit next to her. The fight going on in Vince's body and mind was between loyalty to his old friend, the rat, and his cupidity for the wronged young lady with the bare breast. The young lady seemed to be winning, hands down.

"Take off your shoes and socks," Barbie ordered. Vince obeyed with pleasure.

She was becoming very excited. Perhaps revenge was a powerful aphrodisiac. Whatever it was, the expression "revenge is sweet" played through her mind.

And Barbie, forthwith, took deep, satisfying revenge on her former boyfriend.

She took off the rest of her clothes while Vince watched enthralled. She asked him to stand up. He willingly complied.

Barbie took Vince's belt off, unbuttoned his pants button and pulled down his zipper. He was already hard, as she could see. She managed to get his shorts off around the massive hardon.

"Now take off your shirt and undershirt."

He readily complied.

Barbie had never seen male muscles like these before. Biceps, pectorals, the sixpack of his abs.

"Now lay down that gorgeous hunk of a body on that bed," she ordered.

He lay down with a lopsided grin.

"Spread your legs," she said.

He did.

She approached him from below.

He didn't watch, just staring at the ceiling to await whatever was going to happen.

He gave an involuntary start as he felt her moist lips encircling his balls. But he didn't give a yelp. He *was* aware of the couple in the next room.

She arose, climbed over him, and lowered her cunt down onto his mouth.

"I'm already wet for you, Handsome," she said. "But I want you to lick my cunt so it's even juicier. I want to be damper and then have you fuck my brains out. But quietly, Stud. Let's not disturb your buddy and his boss-lady."

After they had both come with a silent bang, she stood up, and he rose beside her. She motioned for him to follow her to the door. She was curious to see what was happening with the man who had wronged her so.

Again, peeking around the door into the livingroom, Barbie and Vince, unobserved, took a good look at what Jimmy and his boss lady were doing.

As it happened, Jimmy was demonstrating his expertise in what Doctor Morris referred to as "Number Eleven."

A while later, Barbie entered the livingroom with Vince following her.

Both Jimmy and his boss lady were by then fully dressed and sitting on the sofa.

Jimmy was nonplussed and couldn't for the life of him make any kind of introduction. Barbie took the initiative.

"I am Barbie Crown, Jimmy's *ex*-girlfriend."

"And I am Vince Collins, Jimmy's best friend."

Mrs. Hammerschmidt extended her hand first to Barbie and then to Vince.

"And I am Velma Hammerschmidt. James works for me."

She gave Barbie only the slightest attention. But she took her time looking Vince up and down.

"Well, Mr. Collins," she said. "Do you happen to be currently employed?"

"No, Mrs. Hammerschmidt," Vince replied. "I am not. As a matter of fact, I am currently seeking employment."

"Well, well," the lady said. "It so happens that we have a job opening at CIMCO. I think you might just qualify splendidly. Might you be free Monday morning to come down to my office for an interview? At, say, ten o'clock?"

"I would be honored," Vince responded very courteously.

Mrs. Hammerschmidt, Barbie, and Vince all left the apartment together after Barbie and Vince had put their clothes back on.

Jimmy simply stood there in his livingroom, flabbergasted.

There was no doubt in his mind that Vince would soon be 'interviewed' by Mrs. Hammerschmidt at home after he got hired on Monday. He went over Vince's qualities in his mind: handsome, buff, goes to the gym, takes night classes, hung…

It occurred to him that he, himself, might lose Barbie, Chastity, and Mrs. Hammerschmidt.

The coffee he had brewed earlier was still in the pot in the kitchen. There were still a few Krispy Kreem donuts in the box.

He went into the kitchen, poured himself a cup of coffee, and bit into a donut.

"On the other hand," he thought. "I think I made a good impression on Mrs. Hammerschmidt. Maybe everything will turn out okay."

PART THREE

SEXUAL CONGRESS

SEXUAL CONGRESS

Albert and I run this specialized restaurant here in Sacramento. It's called Cupid's Nest.

Oh, oh! There I go calling him Albert. He's my husband, and when I married him, he was still Albert. But he wants everyone to call him François now. You know…because he's maitre d' and all. I keep forgetting, so that's how "Albert" slipped out.

Anyhoo! Cupid's Nest isn't just any old restaurant. It has only private dining rooms. Five of them. Each one has a table and chairs, of course. There are two doors to each room, one the main entrance for the guests from the reception area, and another, a service door, for the servers, leading to the corridor to the kitchen. There's a sideboard in each dining room, to serve from, and a wheeled service cart to bring food and beverages to the table or the bed. Oh, yes. That's one way our restaurant is different from most others. Unlike lots of eating places, each of our dining rooms has a king-sized Murphy bed in it. Like, it folds right up into the wall, but is usually pulled down when our customers get into a romantic mood. If you know what I mean.

We refer to each of our private rooms by a letter name. Like there's Dining Room C. Now you try to think of two body parts that start with C, and you'll know what François (there, I said his name right) had in mind when he named it.

Then, there's Dining Room F. It doesn't take too much imagination to know what François had in mind there.

Of course, there's Q. That's for same-sex couples, as you've already guessed.

And so on, for Rooms P and X. You can fill in the blanks yourself. I've got to get on with my story.

Most of the customers (François calls them clients or guests) are bigshot politicians, lobbyists, or other political types. A really high class bunch. And Jason, he's our chef, prepares really high class food. And our wine cellar has the best wine money can buy. You get the picture.

In addition to François and me and Jason, we have another waiter who we call in when we have more than two dining rooms going.

Well, this one day I want to tell you about was a Friday in May. It was four in the afternoon and Al…François and I were in Room C. We don't open the joint for customers…clients… until six. So we had the room to ourselves. The Murphy bed was pulled down, and François (See, I'm saying it the way he likes it said) and I were sitting on the edge of the bed.

François loves what he calls a matinee. And I'm just crazy about matinees. So, I knew what to expect.

François pulls me close to him, hums a little tune (Don't ask me why. He just did.) and begins nibbling on my earlobe. That is often the beginning of what François calls the hors d'oeuvres. He thinks of love making as a banquet. And we both love banquets, and relish the hors d'oeuvres.

"Mmmm…," I moan, as his tongue playfully examines my ear. "I like that."

That seemed to be his cue to start nibbling at my neck. As his skillful hands played across my chest I felt new tingles. As he kept nibbling at my neck erotic trembles coursed through my body. His small white teeth scraped at the sensitive skin under my chin. Every nibble and scrape sent vibrations all through me. Heaven!

François looked deep into my eyes, and then his lips claimed mine.

Our lips met, tasted, sucked, and consumed each other.

He laid his hand gently on my thigh. I deftly unzipped his pants fly. He had his hand cupped around my pussy. I separated the edges of the fly of his boxer shorts so his prick could emerge. It was hard as a rock. He sucked his finger to coat it with spit so it could slip up my hole and hit my G-spot. I slipped down and moistened his pecker head.

And what happens? There was a knock on the front door to the restaurant. Not just a knock, a pounding. A beating. A banging we could not ignore.

As hot and bothered as we were, we still couldn't ignore the racket.

"What the Hell," François shrugged. "I'd better go see what's going on out there."

François had a Hell of a time getting his engorged dick back into his pants and getting re-zipped. I gave my clit a little massage and had to will myself to stop fluffing off. But business is business.

We left the dining room and crept stealthily towards the front door. The loud beating had not abated. We peeked out the side window, so we could see out and the intruder could not see in.

"Oh, damn!" François muttered. "It's one of our regulars…Ken Carlton. The Republican assemblyman."

"Are you going to let him in?" I asked naïvely.

"Of course not," he answered. "It's not business hours. He has no reason to believe we're in here. He can come back when we're good and ready. And, come back he will. He needs our little nest here if he wants to get his horny needs met. He'll give up pretty soon."

François was right. After a few more frustrated knocks, Assembyman Carlton stamped his foot, uttered a mild oath, got back on the sidewalk, and stalked up the street.

But, François and I didn't go back to continue with the hors d'oeuvres. The mood had been broken.

We sat down on a bench in the reception area.

"That Carlton dude," he said. "He's the one who likes to get his butt whacked, isn't he?"

"Assemblyman Carlton is into what he calls 'pit-a-pat.' But what I would call it is spanking," I replied. "When we're in a hallway, or anywhere that he thinks is at least semi-private, he lifts my skirt."

"And encounters your bare butt," François interjected.

"And encounters my bare butt," I confirmed. "Then he gives me one, two, …even up to four real hard slaps with the palm of his hand."

"And what's your reaction to that?"

"Oh, it tingles real good."

"And that's it?"

"Of course not, silly. I've told you all this before. So you already know."

"But I love to hear it. Tell me what happens then."

"The Assemblyman loosens his belt, unzips his fly, lowers his pants, and moons me."

"Not too dignified for a respectable legislator," François said, as though disapproving. But with a wide, lascivious grin on his face.

"It's my opinion that his posterior is one of his better features," I responded. "So with that rump sticking up at me, I haul off and give him as many hard smacks as I can with my open palm. I don't let up until my hand is so red and sore I can't do it any more. And the Assemblyman is going 'Ooh, aah' under his breath."

"What then"

"He turns towards me and flashes his hard dick at me."

"And what do you do then?"

"I lick my finger, run it up my cunt, and then let him lick my finger."

"And then what?"

"He pulls up his pants, zips up, and hands me twenty dollar bills."

"Now, what I want to know, Sweetie, is this. I never see any of that 'tip' money you get. How much does it amount to?"

"That's *my* secret," I say with a wink. "It's not 'tip money.' It's 'slap and flash money.' And I'm saving it to buy something nice."

"Like?"

"Sexy underwear at Victoria's Secret. To model for you at night after our day's work here is done."

"But, tell me, Chérie. Ball park figure. How much do you get in 'slap and flash' money.'"

"Depends," I say mischievously.

"Depends on what?"

"Never mind," I say. "That's enough about him, Hon. He's not the man in my life. You are."

François gave me a gentle pat on the ass. Not a slap. Definitely a love pat..

"You bet I am," he said in that suggestive voice of his.

I brushed his hand away and said in a petulant voice, "Yes, you are the only man in my life…ever. But you…you were married twice before."

François didn't answer. But he did nod sheepishly in agreement.

I pressed right on. "I hope you didn't love those other wives as much as you love me."

He managed to pat me on the ass again. It made me shiver with delight.

I snuggled up to him.

"Not even close," he said. "You are the only woman I've ever known who is such a wonderful playmate in bed."

I had to laugh. François is very fond of a toss in the hay.

"I'll bet you said the same thing to your previous wives," I ventured.

"Never. And besides, all that's in the distant past. I'm a two-time widower. My previous wives have met their reward." He looked up towards the ceiling, as though he were a lot more pious than I knew him to be.

"So, there's just you, me, and our incredible love life," he said as he ran his finger up my leg and rubbed my wet cunt.

Just then, someone was at the door again, pounding furiously.

"Damn!" François exclaimed. "I guess I've got to go check out what he's after, or he just won't go away.

We both straightened up our clothes to make ourselves more presentable

François opened the door. And standing there was *not* Republican Assemblyman Ken Carlton, but Democratic Senator Ron Plank. The senator had never been to Cupid's Nest before, but I recognized him anyway. His face was on television and in the newspaper enough that you'd think he was someone important. Like a rock star.

We stepped back so the senator could come in. Even though it was François who opened the door, it was me the gentleman stared at. He gave me the once-over, apparently memorizing every curve and line of my body. I could tell he liked what he saw. Suddenly, when he was aware that we were watching his visual examination of my perky orbs, he cleared his throat.

"Ahem," he said, glancing back and forth between François and me. "I was looking for the maitre d'."

"And here I am, Senator Plank," François answered.

The senator looked surprised.

"Do you know me?" he asked.

"The majority leader of the Senate? But of course I know you. You are more famous than the governor."

François can lay it on a bit thick. But all our customers seem to like their egos massaged. And François can give a great rub. Believe me.

While François was warming up Senator Plank, I quietly stole away from the scene and took refuge in a side room where I could overhear what was going on without diverting the customer's thoughts with my curves.

François continued on.

"Despite your fame, Senator, any visits by you to our establishment will go un-noticed by the world. Cupid's Nest is the most discreet spot on earth. We are hosts to nearly every dignitary in Sacramento, foreign and domestic.

And never, ever, has the outside world received intelligence of our clientele. Even the press corps is mum about what goes on here. We host them, too, of course. Our motto is "What happens at Cupid's Nest *stays* at Cupid's Nest."

François had stolen that line from a television commercial about Las Vegas. But he uses it as though it's his very own invention.

I could tell the senator was impressed by the way he cleared his throat. François is good at schmoozing. He went right on.

"Even if you were not the most famous person in the capital, I still would have known you as soon as I saw you."

"How so?" Senator Plank asked.

"I have had the pleasure and the honor of serving you before."

"I believe you are mistaken there, Sir," the senator corrected. "I assure you, this is the first time I have visited your establishment."

"Oh, I'm aware of that, Senator. It wasn't here that I served you. It was at the Fat City Steakhouse."

The senator harrumphed, looking for a word, and then recovered.

"Of course, of course. I didn't recognize you in this context. But now, I do remember you. But I can't place the name."

"It is François, Sir. I was the assistant maitre d' at Fat City."

"Yes, yes. But I still can't recall that as your name."

"I'm called François," my husband answered, trying to give it a French accent.

"François, François? It doesn't quite…"

"Ring a bell?" François finished the thought for him. "The reason for that is that I was still using the name my parents gave me."

"Refresh my memory," Senator Plank said, somewhat bemused.

"It was Albert, Sir," my hubby informed him. "Albert W. Einstein. The 'W' was so no one would confuse me with the…"

For the first time, the senator loosened up and chuckled.

"A clever ploy on their part. Otherwise, I might have thought you were the other one. The one with all the hair."

Senator Plank guffawed. I peeked around the corner. François smiled, but did not appear particularly amused. With all his dignity showing, François continued on.

"I felt that bearing the name Albert Einstein kept me stuck as assistant maitre d'. So when I came here to Cupid's Nest as *the* maitre d', I changed my name to François."

"That's funny," Senator Plank laughed. "You don't look…French."

And with that, he laughed so hard I had to peek around the corner to see him. He turned red as a beet, and tears were running down his face.

François did not laugh, but answered haughtily, "Well, I try to act as snooty as possible to overcome that."

The senator's laughter turned into a coughing spree that began to concern me.

At last he gained control.

"My word," he said. "I do now remember you quite well. I even remember that you mentioned having a wife back then."

"Yes sir. She's now one of my former wives. I had one before her. And I have remarried since her as well."

"It comes back to me now," the senator recalled. "I believe you said that the wife you had there was in…what was it? Oh, yes. That she was in guided missiles."

"Yes, she was a secretary in a guided missile plant in Mountain View."

"And what happened?"

"One day she…just flew off."

That set off a new round of laughter on the senator's part.

"She left you?"

I had to peek at them again. François looked heavenward.

"Dead," he said. "Dead as a drowned rat."

The senator was taken aback.

"'Drowned rat' did you say?"

"A figure of speech, Senator. Bless her soul. Gone to the great beyond."

"You say she was your second wife. Your first…?"

"Worked in a ceramics plant."

The senator was now full of good spirits. Between gasps of laughter he said, "Would you say she was quite a dish?"

Still quite serious and dignified, François said, "Yes, Sir. She was. But her end was tragic, too."

Senator Plank playfully asked, "Cracked or broken?"

I was still watching as François, with a sad look on his face, pointed up towards the ceiling.

"Up there with the other one."

"Sad, sad story," Senator Plank said, trying unsuccessfully to look mournful.

"Yes, indeed. Isn't it? But Senator, I'm sure you didn't come here to discuss my private life. May I presume you came to inquire about the amenities of our boutique restaurant?"

"Exactly," the senator agreed.

François gave him the spiel: "We cater to gentlemen who are seeking a quiet, elegant dinner in the company of a lovely companion. And our chef, Jason, is one of the finest chefs in Sacramento. But, unlike other restaurants, we have five private dining rooms. And each one with a Murphy bed, king size, that pulls down from the wall. That is, of course, for post-prandial... relaxation. May I show you one? As it happens, the bed is pulled down at present in Dining Room C."

"Yes, Alb...François. I would very much like to see the amenities."

"Walk this way, then, Sir," François said.

"If I could walk that way," the senator joked. "I could pass for a maitre d' myself."

He began to laugh at his joke, turning red again. But he regained his composure as he followed François to Room C.

I skedaddled over to the hidden corridor.

Yes, we have a corridor the customers know nothing about. From inside that corridor, there are peepholes into all five dining rooms. Hubby and I get loads of kicks peeking in at the variety of sexual activities carried on in the beds – usually after dinner, but sometimes before even the first course is served.

I saw François and Senator Plank enter the room as I spied through the peephole. The senator's eyes lit up when he saw the bed.

"Would the senator care to test the springs?" François asked.

"Yes, indeed. The young lady I have invited *does*, I believe, relish her comfort."

Senator Plank lay down on the bed and actually flopped about.

"Quite satisfactory, François."

"Shall we reserve this room for you and your companion?"

"Absolutely!"

I was pleased. I thought it would be quite a sight to watch the Senate majority leader frolicking about in that bed with a girlfriend. Working here is *so* much fun.

"What time may we be expecting you, Sir?"

"Eight o'clock would be perfect."

"Eight o'clock it is. Is there anything else, Sir?"

"The food..."

"Put your mind at rest, Senator Plank. I remember your tastes from my Fat City days. Food, service, amenities... All will be impeccable."

"I'll leave it in your capable hands then…François."

There was a knock on the front door. I rushed around to see who was there. And it was Assemblyman Carlton, who had disturbed the games François and I had been playing earlier. I let him in.

"Oh, Tracy!" he exclaimed. "Great to see you." He looked around furtively. "Is anyone around close?"

I wiggled my ass at him in reply. He raised my skirt and gave me a couple of smart slaps. Then he lowered his pants, and I gave him a spanking that turned his cheeks purple.

He stood up, and grabbed his hard dick, and gave it a few jerks.

I stuck my wet finger up my cunt and let him lick the finger, like always.

He pulled his pants back up rapidly. I waited for him to respond. I wasn't disappointed as he slipped me some bills.

Just then, François and Senator Plank were entering the reception area. When the assemblyman and the senator caught sight of each other, they burst out laughing.

François and I know when to withdraw from a room. And we also know where we can go to spy on what's going on in the room we have left. We were out of there. But, of course, within earshot.

Assemblyman Carlton was the first one to speak.

"Ron Plank! The distinguished Senate majority leader. What are *you* doing here, you rascal? Planning a caucus?"

"Well, well, well," Plank responded. "If it isn't the Speaker of the Assembly. How are you doing, Ken? Or, may I ask, *what* are you doing… here?"

"At Cupid's Nest? I imagine the same thing *you* are doing. Making preparations for a romantic dinner for two. Champagne…dessert. I think good Republicans and Democrats all agree to vote for dessert – dessert in bed."

"Hey, Ron," Carlton asked jovially. "You got a minute?"

"Yeah?"

"I think we ought to go sit down and have a…caucus. We seem to have similar agendas here."

Plank nodded in agreement. "Sure. I have the time. Where do you suggest we go to sit?"

"Have you seen Dining Room C?"

"Sure. I was just in there."

"Then you know it has a table and a couple of chairs."

"And a bed!"

"Yep. A bed for a little sporting after dinner. Or even sometimes before. But let's go sit down there at the table and have ourselves a little confab."

"Agreed," the senator said.

As the two gentlemen headed for Room C, François and I rushed to the secret corridor so we could watch and hear the distinguished gentlemen in their discussion.

François manned one peephole, and I stood right next to him at the adjacent one. François likes physical contact while we look in on our customers. And so do I.

As the two legislators entered Room C, we were in position.

François began running the palm of his right hand in circles around my ass. I purred, but too softly to be heard. Just enough to let François know I was happy with what he was doing.

I relaxed into the warm feeling as François watched and listened to the discussion in the dining room.

I was listening, too. But as I listened, I had unzipped François' fly, went down on my knees, and engaged in giving him a blow job.

He gave a little gasp as he came in my mouth.

But it was quiet enough that the gasp couldn't be heard in the other room.

Here's what we heard while I was entertaining François and myself.

Both men were laughing as they settled into their chairs.

"If *you* come to this place," Plank was saying. "It must be true that it's safe to cavort here unobserved by the outside world. The maitre d' told me that what happens at Cupid's Nest stays at Cupid's Nest."

"You can bank on it," Carlton answered.

"It would completely do me in if my wife found out…"

Carlton pretended to be shocked. "You're planning to cheat on your *wife?*"

"You're shocked, Ken?"

"What shocks me is that despite our political differences, we are two peas in a pod. I'd be in really hot water myself if my wife knew about the dates I have here in this establishment."

This was getting really good. Next to watching our customers through the peepholes, listening to them when they think they are not being overheard ranks a close second. People watching and people listening aren't as good as sex. But they are great fun nonetheless.

Listening to the two top politicos in the state discussing their plans for seduction, and how they would be cheating on their wives was a real kick.

Ken Carlton was probing his companion for information.

"So, Ron. Do you have a real hot one on the line for tonight?"

"The hook's in her mouth. All I have to do now is reel her in."

"Cupid's Nest is the place to do it. Trust me. I know."

"So I've gathered."

Assemblyman Carlton wanted to know more.

"Then you're sure you can land her that easy?"

Sen. Plank got serious, and a trifle huffy.

"She's not what you seem to be thinking, Ken. She's a very high class lady. Very sophisticated."

"One of our local society ladies?"

"Oh, no," Sen. Plank protested. "Not local. I don't fish in my own pond."

"I quite agree with you. My companion for the evening is also a very fine, upstanding society lady. And, like yours, an out-of-towner. Here to enjoy the rush of power – being with the speaker of the assembly and all. Political power does have its ancillary benefits. Doesn't it?"

Both men chuckled, and I could see that François was suppressing a laugh as well. So, standing side by side, François and I witnessed the grave discussion in the next room between two of the most powerful men in the state – possibly in the whole country.

Assemblyman Carlton continued to lead his Democrat friend on.

"Tell me more about your…catch."

"She's a widow. But a merry one. Her husband was killed over there in the war."

"Too bad. And since his demise, has she engaged in any little compensatory skirmishes herself?"

"Not at all, my friend. She's been as chaste as the driven snow since… the tragic event."

"How did you happen to meet her, Ron?"

"The lady happens to have a rich old aunt who lives here in town. Well, yesterday, you recall, it was raining."

"Quite a storm," Ken responded.

I hope you don't mind if I call them by their first names now – Ron and Ken. I felt I was getting to know them well enough by then to think of them more familiarly.

Ron continued his story. "I was stupid enough to get caught outside without my umbrella. I got soaked. And what do you know? This knock-out of a woman happened to be returning to her aunt's house. She took pity on me.

'Would you care to share my umbrella, Sir?' she asked."

"Right out of the clear blue sky? I mean…," Ken interjected, jokingly.

Ron didn't seem to know whether Ken was pulling his leg or not. But he continued on in his serious vein.

"I know what you mean, Ken. But, yes. Just like that. As innocent as can be. Even though she's sophisticated, she's naïve too."

Ken congratulated his companion, which led Ron into inquiring about his date for the evening.

"She's quite a lady," Ken replied. "And my story isn't too unlike your own. As you so eloquently remarked, we do appear to be two peas in a pod."

"In affairs of the heart…yes. But politically?"

"On opposite sides of the spectrum," Ron affirmed. "But tell me more about your catch."

I was fascinated by their discussion.

Ken was explaining about the lady friend he would be bringing to our restaurant that evening.

"She's hitched," he explained.

"Married?" Ron exclaimed, but not with surprise.

"Not only married, but to an elderly husband who keeps a very tight rein on her."

"All the more fun," Ron chuckled. "Put one over on the old fool."

Both men laughed.

"How is she able to get away from him tonight?" Ron asked.

"The geezer's gone off to San Diego to an AARP meeting. He sent her here to Sacramento to be watched over by a spinster sister."

"And this sister-in-law of your paramour?"

"Does nothing but watch television all the time. She won't even know my date is gone when she joins me this evening."

"Putting one over on the geezer and the geezer-ess," Ron laughed.

The two men chuckled together. And François silently joined their mirth.

Ron asked, "How did you meet this…tomato?"

"She was at the Community Center Theater. She had sneaked off there to a jazz concert while the old girl was watching the Weather Channel."

"And…?"

"And, the lady happened to be in the seat next to me. She had somehow lost her program and asked if she could share mine. But not forward in the least, you understand. Not as though she were coming on to me. Quite the contrary."

I could see the doubt in Ron's eyes. Ken didn't catch it.

Ken was continuing his description:

"We ended up talking during intermission, and went to the Sutter Grill for a cocktail after the concert. She told me all about her husband being away, and her sister-in-law, and everything. I invited her to dinner here for tonight. She properly refused, again and again. But I wore her down."

"They don't call you Speaker of the Assembly for nothing," Ron joked.

Ken said he thought he would have had to use his speaking abilities to get out of the house and away from his wife. As it turned out, he was in luck.

"My wife solved my problem. She came to me teary-eyed. She had received a phone call from her sister in Pasadena. Their aged aunt has terrible health problems and my wife has to go down there often. So she had to catch a plane this afternoon, which leaves me free to party tonight."

"A likely story," I thought

Ron was saying that he had similar luck with his wife.

"She also has a failing aunt she has to go see regularly. Up in Seattle. It's always some damned thing or other. Fortunately for me. This time the old bat came down with pneumonia. So wifey dear is already on the road to go there and pat her hand."

"Wow!" Ken said. "We certainly are a couple of lucky dogs."

"Say," Ron said. "I was just struck with a great idea."

"What?"

"Why don't you and your...date join us this evening?"

"Join you?" Ken replied, the surprise showing in his voice.

Ron explained his idea.

"It might make the evening seem more convivial and less strained at the beginning. Naturally, when it's *dessert* time, François can provide separate rooms...and beds."

Ken was agreeable to the idea.

"Okay, Ron. Let's all four of us meet right here in Dining Room C tonight. I'll arrange for François to keep Room F, and its bed, ready for my date and me at dessert time."

The legislators left, laughing jovially, hands on each other's shoulders.

Sure enough, about an hour later, while François and I were setting up the rooms for the evening, Ken called to explain that there would be four of them in Room C until dessert time. I was the one who took the call. He said that he wanted Room F for himself and his date after the main course.

Unfortunately, Room F was already reserved. As a matter of fact, all the dining rooms were reserved for that evening except Q. There were no same-sex reservations for the evening. So we could change the environment in the room to "straight" by the time he and his date arrived.

"No problem," the Speaker said. "I just don't want any pictures on the wall that might suggest that I go for guys."

I assured him the room would be decorated in a manner that would enhance the after-dinner drinks and dessert. He told me I was a doll, and would look forward to an appetizer from me before his date arrived.

As you know, he was referring to his penchant for a few slaps on his ass, and on mine.

When I told François that the arrangement was made, he chuckled. "You and I have to be there. I'll have Jake do all the serving in Rooms F, P, and X. We won't want to miss a thing with these two legislators."

Jake is the reserve waiter who does a lot of the serving at our place. I was happy that François and I could give our full attention to our distinguished guests of the evening.

That evening, at quarter to eight, Ken arrived at our restaurant. At the time, I was just finishing setting up the champagne bucket and the hors d'oeuvres on the sidebar. François led Ken to Room C and left him with me.

Ken was clearly anxious for his appetizer, what he called his "pit-a-pat". He didn't have to raise my skirt. I raised it myself, exposing my rosy cheeks for his expectant palm.

"Smack!"

And smack two, three, and four.

Which meant "Tingle, tingle, tingle, ouch!"

He dropped his pants and drawers, and I was determined to give him tit for tat. (Well, not exactly 'tit.' Not 'tat' either. More like 'slap.')

"Smack!"

And two, three, four, and five.

Boy, did my hand ever ache. As red as my palm was, the assemblyman's butt was much, much rosier.

I responded by pulling up my skirt and mooning him. Damned if he didn't bend over and kiss my ass. Not the cheeks – the asshole itself. Jeesh! What a creepy feeling that was.

"Wow!" he exclaimed. "What a tasty way to begin the evening."

He had pulled up his pants and zipped his fly just before François re-entered the room.

"Did I hear something falling in here?" my hubby asked, playing dumb.

"Yes," I whispered to him. "More twenty dollar bills than you could imagine."

"Assemblyman Carlton," he said in his snootiest tone. "Would you care to inspect Room Q?"

"Yes," was the reply. "I'd like to see that the décor is appropriate for the occasion."

"Then, walk this way," François said.

And, as nearly always, Ken came back with a joke very like the one Ron made earlier in the day. François sets the men up on purpose so they can feel witty. It's a maitre d' thing.

Just before eight o'clock, I went out to the reception area. I had no sooner taken my place behind the reception desk than Ron entered. He is an imposing figure. He's one of the more handsome senators in the capitol. He greeted me with a smile.

"Good evening...Tracy?"

I nodded, pleased that he had remembered my name right.

He took a watch out of his vest pocket and pointed the face toward me.

"Eight o'clock," he said. "Right on the dot. I hope the lady has not yet arrived."

"No young lady yet, Senator," I informed him. "But just coming in the door right now there is a most attractive woman. Could that be the person you're entertaining at our Cupid's Nest this evening?"

He turned around and beamed.

"Daisy!" the senator exclaimed. "I just got here myself. Looks like we're both punctual people."

"Oh," Daisy answered. "I'm the kind of woman who always likes to come on time."

I smirked at that. Ron looked flustered, and Daisy lowered her eyes in a maidenly manner.

"François is attending to another guest," I said. "May I lead you to your dining room?"

"Certainly," Ron said. "Come along dear," he invited his new girlfriend.

"Just walk this way," I said, copying François' line.

"If I walked that way, I'd need to dust talcum powder between my legs," Daisy said quietly to me. Ron didn't hear her. I nearly cracked up.

When we arrived at Room C, there was Veuve Clicquot champagne in the wine bucket. There were four champagne flutes on the table, and the tray was loaded with canapés.

"Would you like me to uncork the champagne bottle?" I asked. "I take care of those things when François is not available."

"Yes, please," Ron said.

The Murphy bed was pulled down.

"Oh, lookie!" Daisy squealed. "A bed! Why in the world would they put a bed in a dining room?"

She was playing Little Miss Innocent to a tee. But she didn't have me convinced, I'll tell you.

I popped the cork off the bottle just then, which caused the two of them to jump. Then Daisy fanned herself with her hand and sat on the bed.

"Mercy," she said. "That gave me quite a start."

Ron sat down beside her and patted her on the shoulder.

"There, there, my dear. Are you all right?"

"Oh, yes…Senator. I'll be all right."

I brought them their champagne as they settled comfortably on the edge of the bed. Then I wheeled the serving wagon over to them and set the champagne bottle and the hors d'oeuvres on it. There was a little silver bell on the wagon.

"If there's anything you want, just ring this bell," I told them.

I eased out the door and hurried as fast as I could to get to the secret corridor to see how this senator and his lady operated. When I got to the peephole, they were sipping their champagne and sampling the hors d'oeuvres.

"Oh, Senator," Daisy was saying. "I just don't feel right about this. Sitting in a strange room, with a strange man, on a strange bed. And sipping champagne."

"Tut, tut, my dear," Ron replied. "First off, no 'Senator' here. Please call me 'Ron.' And there's nothing really strange. It's all very proper, I assure you."

He pecked her on the cheek. She didn't resist. But she didn't really encourage him either.

"It's just that I've never done anything like this before in my life.

What would *he* think?" Daisy asked demurely.

Ron looked surprised. "He?! He who?"

Daisy pointed Heaven-ward.

"Oh," Ron said. "Him!" He pointed upward, too. "I'm sure he's happy stroking his harp away and has his mind on other things. I'm sure he's stroking something, anyway."

She looked relieved. "Oh, I do so hope you're right."

"I'm sure I'm right," he said, putting his glass on the serving tray. She didn't respond to his 'stroking' joke. He patted her thigh in a paternal way. "You just must relax. Let me pour you a bit more champagne. It's really a very nice wine, don't you think?"

He poured more champagne into her glass, and then returned his hand to her thigh. She didn't object.

As Daisy continued to sip her champagne, his hand traced a course up and down her thigh. Before too long his hand was caressing her cunt. She pretended not to notice, but her shudders of pleasure revealed that she was far from resisting his advances.

"You are a very beautiful woman," the senator said softly. "You mustn't shut yourself off from the world."

She sipped, and purred, and sipped, and purred.

"I'm afraid this champagne is going to my head," she apologized.

The champagne may have been going to her head. That's not where Ron's hand was. It was giving a gentle massage to her pussy. She continued to sip, as though unaware of the liberty.

"Oh," she cooed. "Look what we have here. Could I just take a little nibble of these delightful hors d'oeuvres?"

And, at that moment, all three of us, Daisy, Ron, and I heard a sound in the hallway behind them.

It looked to me as though one of the senator's fingers had sunk up into the hole right at par when there was the sound of someone approaching the door.

Ken's form outlined the doorway.

Daisy said, "We need to get out of here and straighten up our clothes."

And as Ken was entering the room, Ron and Daisy beat a hasty retreat out the service door as Ken gained full entrance to the room.

They just made it out of the room as Ken was opening the door.

"Right in here," he was saying.

When they entered, the room was empty of its former occupants.

107

His date for the evening was hanging on his arm. And she had a pair of boobs that were absolute knockouts. He really had a beaut on his hands.

"Oh, Assemblyman," she was saying. "This is the private dining room you were telling me about?"

"No more of that 'Assemblyman' talk out of *you*, young lady. This is an informal situation. Between us, it's Ken and Marge from now on."

"If you say so…Ken," Marge answered coyly.

She looked around.

"What a funny dining room," she exclaimed. "Why is there a bed in here?"

"In case you get tired. The management here thinks of everything."

"Oh, I see," she said. "Let's sit down and rest, then."

They sat on the edge of the bed.

"How thoughtful," she said. "And look! A cart with some wine and some glasses next to the bed. It looks like someone's been in here drinking."

"Probably the other couple."

"*What* other couple?"

"I was about to tell you, Marge," the assemblyman explained. "We'll be joined by another couple. That is, if that's all right with you."

"If they're friends of yours, I suppose it's all right."

"Oh, yes. Very fine, sophisticated people. You will be absolutely amazed at who will be joining us. It's a surprise celebrity."

"Oh, goodie," she said. "I love surprises. And look, the champagne. It's Veuve Clicquot. My very favorite. Shall we test it?"

Ken filled the two clean flutes with the wine.

"Oh, I'm just crazy about the bubbly, aren't you?" Marge enthused. "And look at all these lovely hors d'oeuvres. I just know I'm going to love it here."

As he handed her a glass, Ken said, "Drink up, my dear. There's more where this came from."

They clicked their glasses. As they did so, a bit of the champagne spilled onto the front of his pants and some spilled on her blouse. If you ask *me,* they did it on purpose. These two seemed to know exactly what they were doing.

"Oh, dear," Marge sighed. "I seem to have wasted some of this delicious champagne. I spilled it on my blouse."

"Perhaps you should take off the blouse so we can remedy the situation," the speaker suggested.

"What a good idea," she said as he helped her out of the blouse.

As I suspected from the jiggle as she entered the room, there was no brassiere under that blouse. And those proud golden hooters were unleashed on the room.

Ken was dumbstruck by what he saw. When he regained his composure he found just the right thing to say.

"Oh, oh," Ken said. "There's still some wine on that breast. Let me lick it off so it doesn't get wasted."

Before you could say 'boo' his tongue was sucking her nipples.

"Wait a minute, Ken," the lady was saying. "You spilled some wine on your pants, too. You'd better take them off so they don't get stained."

"Good idea," he murmured.

Ken slipped off his pants. She bent over and surrounded his peckerhead with avid lips.

And, as luck would have it, just then, we heard Ron in the outer hallway talking to François. I couldn't get what they were saying, but I certainly saw the effect on the loving couple in Room C.

Marge hustled her blouse on. But, she couldn't get it on quite straight. So she rushed out the service door to get out of sight.

Ken got his pants back on, after a bit of fumbling.

Ron burst into the room, full of enthusiasm.

"Aha, Ken," he said. "Here you are."

Ken did his best to look pleased.

François came into the room and checked the champagne bottle. He carried it to the sideboard and picked up the wine bucket.

"I'll be back shortly with another bottle," he announced.

And with bottle and bucket in hand, François went out the service door.

The two legislators were left in the room together. And I was in my observation corridor. What a trip that had been.

Ron was asking where Ken's date was.

"She went to powder her nose. And whatever else she fancies to powder," Ken said, joking his way back to normal.

"How about your date?"

"She went to the powder room, too. The two ladies may meet each other there."

"I guess I'll go to the gents' room myself," Ken said. "I seem to need to wash my hands."

Just minutes later, Daisy entered the room through the main door. She gave Ron a peck on the cheek. He gave her a pat on the ass.

"We certainly had a narrow escape," Ron said.

"Yes," Daisy giggled. "Your friend nearly caught us in what could have been an embarrassing situation. I just wish we'd had a chance to go on with what we were doing a little longer."

Ron nodded his agreement.

"When's dinner?" Daisy asked.

"Very soon now," he answered. "The other couple has already arrived. They'll be back shortly. I think I'd better go see if I can intercept François. I can see we're going to need oysters before long. And I want to be sure he'll be bringing in a couple dozen."

Ron left Daisy in the room to go on his quest for oysters.

He hadn't been gone two minutes when François came into the room through the service door with a new bottle of champagne in an ice bucket.

"Shall I uncork the champagne, Mam'selle?" he asked Daisy.

"Please," she answered, helping herself to some hors d'oeuvres.

François did the honors and left the room with the empty bottle.

François had just left the room when Ron and Ken entered, arm-in-arm.

Ron cleared his throat.

"Ahem, my dear. I would like you to meet my good friend Ken Carlton. You will recognize him from your newspaper reading and the TV news. He is the Speaker…"

Ron never got his sentence finished. Daisy took one look at Ken. Ken took one look at her. And they both let out a scream that could have awakened the dead.

Daisy cried out, "Yikes! Ken! You!!"

Ken was simultaneously bellowing, "Good Lord! Daisy!"

Ron seemed pleased.

"Oh, he said. "What a pleasant surprise. You two have apparently met previously."

Ken was livid. He pointed at Daisy and shouted, "Kindly explain what you are doing in a place like this!"

Daisy shouted right back.

"Me?! What am *I* doing here? That's a laugh. What are *you* doing in a place like this? You louse!"

Ken shot right back, "Your aged aunt in Pasadena must have had some kind of instant miracle cure. You liar!"

But I wasn't confused. I thought the picture was pretty obvious. And pretty hilarious to boot.

Ken hadn't finished unloading his surprise and anger.

"And to think I was sap enough to trust and believe you. When I think of all the times you've pulled that sick aunt routine on me…"

And Daisy was not to be out-shouted.

"Oh, yeah? Try telling me you're not two-timing me here with some cheap floozy."

Ken, politician that he was, took a new tack.

"That's not the point, Daisy. I've caught you here, red-handed, with *him*!"

When he pointed at Ron, Ron ran to the other side of the bed to get out of harm's way. And he tried to calm Ken down.

"Now, now, Ken. You mustn't jump to conclusions…"

Ken turned the discussion more political yet.

"Conclusions?!" he shouted. "It's just about what you could expect from a Democrat. Pretty liberal – making hay with my wife."

Ron hadn't caught on as fast as I did.

"Your *wife*?! You don't mean to tell me…"

Ken was really worked up.

"I don't mean to tell you anything your double-dealing Democrat heart wasn't already aware of. Your party will stoop to…"

Ron came right back at him.

"You leave my party out of this. You Republicans are so paranoid, you…"

And would you believe it? Exactly at that moment, Marge walked into the room. Ron caught sight of her as she entered.

"Marge!?" he shouted in surprise.

Ken was caught in mid-sentence.

In bewilderment, he said, "Who are you calling Marge? Why, you…"

Ron stomped his foot.

"Not you! Stupid!" He pointed at Marge. "Her!"

Every eye turned on Marge. When she saw Ron, she turned livid.

"Ron Plank! Of all people! In a place like this! You certainly have some explaining to do."

Marge pointed at Daisy.

"You've come here to cavort with that…that *tramp*. Haven't you? And it looks like you were having a little threesome, eh? Two men. One woman. I couldn't imagine how kinky you really are."

That flustered Ken and Daisy something awful. I could tell that Ken was very irritated at being suspected of being party to…well, *that* kind of party.

Ron wasn't through with his rage.

"You said you were off to Seattle. Old aunt sick with pneumonia. You lying slut."

Daisy felt like getting her own oar in this.

To Marge, she yelled, "Yeah! Slut!"

Marge was ready to really go at her, tooth and toenail.

"Oh! Slut am I? Trying to steal my husband. I'll show you, you…"

The room was in a hubbub. And I was crying with laughter.

And who should come popping in through the service door, carrying a tray, but François.

"Here are some nice oysters, folks. I thought…"

Daisy stopped dead in her tracks and pointed.

"You! Albert!"

François set the oysters down on the side table and blurted out, "Daisy!" Then, in a subdued tone, he said, "Actually, I'm called François now."

Marge was equally flabbergasted. She pointed.

"You! Albert!"

He could only meekly answer, "I'm François now."

Ron was the first to size up the situation.

"It seems, whether you are Albert or François, you are acquainted with these ladies."

"Actually," he explained. "They are my two ex-wives."

Now, that one hit me like a ton of shit. I stormed out of the secret corridor, circled around into the service corridor, and in seconds I burst into the room.

When François saw me, I thought he was going to faint.

"Is that true, Albert W. Einstein? Are *these* the ex-wives you told me were dead and up in Heaven?"

Both ladies exclaimed together, "Dead?! In Heaven?!"

François said to me, "Look, Honey. I lied to you. I didn't want you to be jealous of my ex-wives. So, I just kind of killed them off."

Our four guests said in unison, "Killed them off?"

I thought it was time to insert some reason into this mess.

"Look! We all seem to have some surprises here. There's no point to getting upset.

"I've learned that my husband lied to me. And each of you found out that not only is your spouse a liar, but also knows *you're* a liar.

"You came here to have a good time. Admit it."

All four of our guests nodded their heads and François looked sheepish.

"Jason has prepared a delicious meal for you. We have some fine wines to go with the food. Jason will keep the food warm. The wine will wait. I say there's just one thing we should *all* do right now."

All five, with one voice, said, "What?"

"I say, let's party. Come on now. All of us. Me and François too."

And party we did. It would be impolitic for me to describe the frolic we had. There was fucking and sucking aplenty involved…and much, much more. Suffice it to say that all political differences were set aside…for the time being.

When our frolic was over, our four guests sat at the table. I served the oysters. François served the wine. And, in due course, we both brought in the succulent dinner our Jason had prepared for our guests.

Later, one couple was in the bed in Room C and the other in Room Q. François and I scurried from one peephole to another to observe who was doing what to whom. And, if you think I'm going to tell you who was doing it to whom, you just don't understand.

What happens at Cupid's Nest *stays* at Cupid's Nest.

PART FOUR

EDUCATING FLAMING MAME

EDUCATING FLAMING MAME

VOICE OF DOC KINKAID

Hi, folks! I'm Doc. Doc Kinkaid from down Avondale way. You might have heard of Avondale? It's in the San Joaquin Valley? That big new oil strike? Yep. That's where I'm from. I have a ranch there, a real nice ranch. Mainly cabbage. You can make a good living raising cabbage.

I never got married. Never had to. There are three cat houses within easy driving distance of my ranch. The one in Hanford's the closest but the girls in Goshen and Dinuba are friendlier. With easy relief that close, who needed a wife? I figured it out once. It's a hell of a lot cheaper buying sex by the piece than tying yourself up with some gal's gonna be nagging at you all the time and holding out on you when you're horny. My buddies Skeeter and Rat, they got married. All they do when they can break loose and get down to the Wrongbranch Saloon to toss a few with me is complain about their old ladies. Who needs *that*?

I don't want you to get the idea that the only loving I ever got back home was from the whores. You see, the whores down our way draw the line at anything even slightly romantic. And besides, it's no fun to always have a sure thing. So there's this Methodist church in the Valley that has what they call a singles club. I used to go there regularly and meet the chicks. I'd date them and see how far I could get with them. Most of the young ladies wouldn't go further than some kissing and a little petting. There are two gals, though, I won't tell you their names, but one of them let me get real, real fresh with her. And that was pretty much the extent of my sex life in the Great San Joaquin Valley.

Now let me tell you something about the way folks are named down Avondale way. Like me, for example. Folks call me Doc. I'm not any kind of doctor. My given name is Douglas. When I was little, I couldn't say Doug too well, and called myself "Doc." Down our way, the name stuck. My good old buddy Schuyler, he became Skeeter. You can see why. No one wants to get stuck with a name like Schuyler. And Rat? He's a little guy. Smallest guy on our high school football team. He was our quarterback and he could run like a rat right through or around the line of the opposing teams. Everyone called him Rat. He was proud of the name and he still is.

Then there's my cousin Bo. He's my first cousin on my daddy's side. Handsomest little devil in the whole damn family. More than handsome. That dude was and is downright pretty, if you ask me. So, my aunt, who studied French in high school, started calling him "Beau." Well, he ended up being called "Bo" of course. In Avondale, his effeminate ways caused the other kids to call him "Bofag." So, as soon as he was out of high school, he hightailed it for Frisco, and changed from a fag to a gay. Good move, I always thought.

Anyhow, to get back to what I wanted to tell you. One day some fellows from Slicker Oil Company called me up and wanted to talk to me. I told them I'd meet them down at the Wrongbranch.

Turned out they wanted to drill in my cabbage patch. At first I said, "Hell no!" Then they told me how much they'd pay me if I let them drill. And I said, "Hell, yes!"

Then they told me what they'd pay me if they ran into the kind of oil their petroleum engineer thought might be lying there under my cabbages. I like to messed my pants. They put a bunch of papers in front of me. I couldn't sign those suckers fast enough.

The day they struck oil, I said to myself, "To Hell with those goddam cabbages" and I headed here to Frisco. I've got to tell you, folks. I'm one rich dude now. And with all this dough, I wanted to learn about the fast life in the big city.

I telephoned my cousin Bo and told him about my good luck. And I told him how I wanted to take my dough up there to Frisco and see what life was like outside the Valley.

Bo congratulated me on my good luck and said he hoped maybe his folks' place might be over that oilfield, too. I agreed. I'm still hoping my uncle and aunt have oil under their turnip ranch. No one's approached them about doing any drilling yet. But you never can tell, can you? Bo said he had a kind of little den in the place where he was living. If I didn't feel I needed too much room, I could move in with him. He said I could stay there free, but, of course, I wouldn't hear of it. So we agreed on a reasonable rent for me to pay him. It wasn't much, but I certainly wasn't going to sponge off Bo.

So I got a ranch management company to look after my ranch and I moved in with Cousin Bo at his apartment on Ford Street in Frisco.

He was right about the den being dinky. But that wasn't really a problem for me. We put his desk in storage, moved in a bed, and it suited me just dandy.

Ford Street is in what they call the Castro District here in the city. It's like a whole separate town nestled right into Frisco.

Castro Street is kind of like Gay Main Street here. The heart of the gay community is centered around Castro Street between Market and Eighteenth. They've got shops, restaurants, bars, theaters, everything you need. And all those institutions are really gay.

I'm not gay myself, but it never bothered me having a gay cousin. So being surrounded by homos doesn't bother me one damned bit.

I don't want to go into telling you about all that stuff I did that everyone does when he first gets to Frisco. You know, the cable cars, Fisherman's Wharf, Golden Gate Park, blah, blah, blah. Yeah, Bo and I did all that. But that wasn't what I was here for.

We went to a lot of Bo's favorite clubs and bars. No one pestered me much. Sure, there were guys who came on to me, but Bo knew just what to say to them to get rid of them and that was that. The music at a lot of the places throbbed so you couldn't hear what anyone else was proposing or propositioning to you anyway.

Some of the clubs were mainly gay. Some were mainly lesbo. But they all seemed tolerant of everyone, even straights like me. Naturally, some enjoyed watching the guys at the Levis 'n' leather bars. It was like Halloween there.

A lot of people wouldn't think so, I guess. But lots of gays are into sports. Bo's as much of a sports fan as I am. I've always watched football on TV and the 49ers are by far my favorite pro team. I'm a real fan. One of the clubs there in the Castro is called Score. And what it is, it's actually a gay sports bar. I really enjoyed that club more than any of the other clubs Bo took me to. Until this one night.

The Niners were playing the Raiders at 3Com. In case you don't know, the Frisco 49ers and the Oakland Raiders are arch rivals. The game was sold out at the stadium, so it got broadcast locally. Bo and I got to the Score early to get a booth, because Bo knew the joint would be packed to watch the game on the big screens.

We got in a booth that had a great view of a screen. The booth was meant to hold six people, but by the time the game started there were eight of us crammed in there.

Bo was on my right side, and a knockout of a chick was on my left. This was the first gal who really raised my interest since I'd arrived in town. I figured the problem would be, she'd be a lesbo, because she'd arrived with another chick, also a real looker. They were holding hands and seemed real interested in each other. So I didn't try to put the moves on her.

It was a good game. The Niners were outplaying the Raiders and all of us at the booth were shouting and cheering and guzzling one beer after another. Except the chicks. They were both drinking white wine. But the gal next to me was putting it down as fast as the rest of us were guzzling.

At the end of the first quarter, the Niners were ahead fourteen points.

The chick's right hand brushed against my leg. It wasn't anything suggestive particularly. Like I say, we were crammed awfully tight into that booth. But still.

Then, the Raiders kicked a field goal. And it was good. When we saw the ball go over the goalpost the gal grabbed my leg.

I looked at her.

"Sorry," she said. "I got a little carried away."

"That's O.K.," I answered. But I began to wonder.

Second quarter the score was fourteen to three. The Raiders had the ball. Kerry Collins tossed the ball to Adkisson. Damned if Adkisson didn't run the ball thirty-five yards to a touchdown!

I knew what I was going to do. I grabbed the chick's thigh.

"Sorry, I got a little carried away, too." I mock apologized.

She winked at me.

Golly! I figured even if she was a lesbo, maybe she swung both ways. I hadn't got laid since I'd been in the city. I'd never done it with a lesbian. But what the Hell? This was worth pursuing.

Before you knew it, she was rubbing my thigh and I was rubbing hers.

Just soft like, you know. Not so anyone would know. But I'd got pretty horny not having had any sex for a while. I had to do something.

I said to my cousin, "Excuse me, Bo. I got to go take a leak."

He and the guy next to him got out of the booth so I could get up. I slipped out, and started for the can. I went on to the can and took care of my business.

I walked back to the booth. No one paid any attention to me. No one, that is, but the gal who'd been sitting beside me.

Bo and the guy next to him got up to let me in. They were intent on the game. The two minute warning was announced, and Oakland had the ball again. They were in field goal position. They sent out their kicker, Kanikowski. As the ball sailed towards the goal post, damned if the gal didn't slip her hand into my lap.

My God! Everyone else in the place was moaning and booing and cussing and I couldn't even concentrate on the game.

The field goal was good.

The gal buzzed in my ear, "What's your name, Honey?"

"Doc," I say. "What's yours?"

"Darlene. Can you give the slip to your boyfriend? I think you and I might find some interesting halftime activities."

Man-o-man! It seemed like she was a lesbian who *could* swing both ways and that she figured I was a gay who could, too. Wow!

Halftime and the score was fourteen-thirteen. The Niners were leading by only one point. Lots of people were heading for the cans. Darlene and I found it possible to get out of the booth.

"I'll see you for the third quarter," I told Bo. He just nodded and headed off to take a leak. Darlene said something to her girlfriend, nodded to the door, and Darlene and I headed out of the saloon together.

"We've got to make this a quickie," she said, taking my hand and leading me across the street. "I want to get back in fifteen minutes. We don't want to miss the third quarter."

Well, a quickie would suit me just fine. Get somewhere fast with this chick, do the deed, and not miss any of the game. How can you beat that for a perfect score? We walked down the street two short blocks, took a right, and she led me up the front steps of an apartment building. She let go of my hand, fished in her purse and pulled out a key.

We entered and walked up a flight of stairs to the second floor.

"We can make it up to my place faster walking than taking the goddam elevator," she explained. She was in a big damned rush, and so was I.

Her apartment was just down the hall two doors.

When we entered her place I scoped it out pretty fast. It was a studio apartment, furnished in pinks and mauves. Big posters of football players, wrestlers and movie stars were on the wall. There was a Murphy bed pulled down. There were bar stools by a passthrough opening. I could see the kitchen on the other side of the passthrough.

There wasn't a door to the kitchenette. Just an open space to walk through. There were two doors to the place other than the entry door. I knew one would lead to a closet and the other to the can. So much for the place.

That babe was deft and efficient. She had my belt whipped off me and the top button of my Levis unbuttoned faster than you could say "Hot damn."

Next thing you know, she was giving me a hummer.

I was one happy dude.

When she finished, I ran my hand real fast up underneath her skirt. She didn't have any panties on. That was the good news.

The bad news was, she wasn't a she at all. She was a he! Darlene started to laugh.

"What did you expect up there, Doc? A ham and cheese sandwich?" he/she asked.

I started to gag. I knew I was going to puke. I pulled my pants up lickety-split and made a dash for the kitchen. I got to the sink just in time and up she came. I barfed up all the Budweiser that was in my stomach. Yuck!

I turned on the water and washed the vomit down the drain.

I staggered back to the other room.

"Sorry," I apologized.

"I kind of thought you might be a virgin," she said.

"She said?" "He said?" What the Hell! I didn't know whether to think "he" or "she."

"Come on, Doc," she said. (I'd decided on "she.") "You had a hell of a time and you know it. Hang around the Castro long enough you'll get used to getting it on with us queens. Get those jeans zipped up, huh? We don't want to miss the second half of the game."

We hurried back to The Score, but we didn't hold hands, believe me. The halftime show had just finished and there were beer and Viagra ads on the screen. Bo and the guy next to him got out of the booth. Darlene got in. I urged Bo to get in then so he'd be next to her. Then I got in and the end guy resumed his place.

For the first time in my life, I found it hard to keep my mind on a football game. Tim Rattay connected with Jason McAddley during the third quarter giving the Niners a more comfortable lead. And they kept that lead through the fourth quarter. The game was exciting enough that there were whole sequences of two or three minutes at a time when my thoughts weren't balancing the charge of that sex experience with Darlene mixed with the horror of having a handful of something that turned my stomach.

When the football game was over, Bo said he was going to hang around for a while. I told him I'd see him back at the place.

Out of force of habit I said a nice goodbye to Darlene. She smiled back at me sweetly. I could see that pretty made-up face. And at the same time, I could remember that yucky feeling of having a handful of cock and balls.

I got back to Bo's apartment and gave myself a real good shower. I wanted to wash away the disgusting part of my experience with Darlene. But I couldn't wash away the pleasure of the sexual part. Man! It really was one Hell of a blow job.

Bo got back to the apartment about an hour and a half later. I was sitting up in the livingroom reading Sports Illustrated.

He sank down into his favorite chair.

"Well, Sport," he said. "What can I say? I guess I should have warned you. But honest to God, I didn't catch what was going on between you and Darlene."

"Do you know Darlene?" I asked.

"I didn't," he answered. "But after you left she and her girlfriend struck up a conversation with me and the guy who was sitting next to me. Guy's name is Max. Max and I went with Darlene and her friend, Polly, to Polly's place. We had a foursome that was pretty wild. Darlene told me what happened to you. I guess I thought you knew about transvestites."

"I'd heard about them," I told him. "But I thought they would look like guys in gal's clothing. I didn't expect they'd be gorgeous with such shapely legs."

"Well," he said, "at least the sex part was pretty good, wasn't it?"

"God, yes," I admitted. "Best cock sucking I ever had."

"Me, too," he told me.

I thought we'd laugh our butts off.

That got me over the blues I'd felt about my experience with Darlene.

Bo said, "Look, Doc. I respect your orientation, and I'm not out to change it. I always appreciated the way you accepted me for who and what I am over in the Valley. I want you to know that I feel the same way about you being straight. I really mean it."

123

I knew he meant it, and appreciated him saying it.

I went on to the den to bed and fell asleep with a smile on my face.

The next morning Bo and I went to the Caffè Luna Plena on Castro for breakfast. Their French toast with fruit compote and mascarpone cream is *really* good. We dawdled over our meal. You don't want to rush a good thing like that.

"I'm going up to Haight-Ashbury to score a dime bag," Bo told me. "Come on along. There are still girls left over from the flower children days up in that district. They're into free love and peace. You might be able to score some action for yourself and kind of cover over some of the shock of last night."

It sounded like a good idea to me.

Haight is the next neighborhood north of Castro, but I found out it's a world away.

Bo parked down by Masonic and we walked along Haight towards Golden Gate Park. The famous psychedelic Summer of Love was held in that neighborhood a few generations back, in the sixties. The leftovers are still hanging around, pathetic geezers and geezerettes panhandling for money to feed their habit. Redheads, blueheads, greenheads, potheads, and hopheads are all over the place. It's a zoo. But just as interesting as the freaks are the tourists who are trying not to gawk at that human zoo.

One thing was definite. There was no way I would let myself get laid by any of the pathetic old crones with the vacant eyes and the wilted flowers in their hair.

"Did you say something about me getting it on with a flower child?" I teased Bo.

"They aren't all old, Doc," Bo assured me. "Check out the one with the spiked blue hair," he said, nodding at a sixteen year old chick wearing a tie-dyed t-shirt and cutoffs.

"I'm not that interested in spending time in the Frisco jail," I answered. "She looks a little young to me."

"Jeez, you're finicky," he laughed. "But I have a plan for tomorrow where we'll find you a female the right age, who's ready and willing, and who'll give you an experience like I guarantee you've never had before."

"Great!" I said. "Tell me about it."

"It's a surprise," Bo answered.

He ducked into a store that sells incense, ratty looking old clothing, and cheap knick-knacks like ash trays that feature pictures of Alcatraz on them. Bo talked to the clerk of the store. The clerk made a call on his cellphone and then told Bo something.

Bo came over to where I was looking at a ceramic statue of Jerry Garcia.

"Wait here a moment, will you?" Bo asked. "I'll be back real soon."

Before I could say "yes," "no," or "what the Hell?" he was out the door. About ten minutes later he was back with a smile on his face. He'd scored a baggie of pot.

I was ready to leave the store but Bo said he had another purchase to make. He went over to the incense counter and ruffled through the merchandise. He chose a couple of sticks of some smell or other. I don't know one incense from another. He also got a kind of gizmo that could hold a half dozen of the sticks at the same time. I guessed he was going to stink up the apartment something fierce. O.K. with me. I figured it must be a big city thing. He paid for his purchases, and we were out of there.

Bo asked me if I'd like some lunch in the neighborhood. I figured I'd never willingly come back there so I might as well get the most out of my one trip.

"Sure," I said. "I haven't completely lost my appetite here in the Haight."

The restaurant Bo liked was down Haight Street about a block from the park. It's a place called Cha Cha Cha. This eatery is set up Caribbean style with fake banana trees, plastic tropical table cloths, and even some goofy looking setups Bo told me were Santería altars. I still don't know what the Hell *those* are.

We ordered from the tapas menu and shared Cajun shrimp, fried calamari, and stuff I'd never seen before and that I don't remember the names of. But I can tell you it was delicious. Bo ordered sangrías to drink with our food and they were good too. It all kind of washed away the tawdriness of what I'd seen so far in the Haight-Ashbury. When we'd finished our meal, we walked back to the car and returned to the Castro.

Bo was having a friend of his over to our place that evening. That's what he got the pot for, and probably the incense as well. We went to Lucky Pierre's Boulangerie down on Hancock and got a bunch of French pastries and a kind of chocolate cake he called a Sachertorte. We went to the Sweet Tooth on Castro and bought a bag of caramel corn there. It seems that Jo, his friend, has a sweet tooth.

I asked him about Jo.

"Bo and Jo," he explained. "That's what our friends call us."

"Joe as in Joseph or Jo as in Josephine?" I asked. Maybe I'd just fallen off the turnip truck, but I was learning a few things about life in the Castro.

"Yeah," was his answer.

I didn't flinch a bit. I'd come to Frisco to learn about life in the big city. I was learning.

We met Jo at seven that evening at the 2223 Restaurant, which happens to be at 2223 Market Street. Jo is about as pretty as Bo, but more wispy, with blond hair that's almost white and pale, and pale skin like he's never been out in the California sun in his life. He has light blue eyes that are kind of dreamy. I liked the guy. He's very quiet, nearly shy. He's polite and kind of academic and highbrow sounding.

Bo ordered drinks for us. I don't know what they were but they were pretty sweet and had pink umbrellas sitting in them. I wasn't too surprised. Bo had told me his friend was into sweets.

Jo ordered grilled pork chops and Bo and I got roast chicken with garlic mashed. Real good. No dessert. We were going to have that back at the apartment.

Jo was interested in my telling him about what Bo was like as a kid, and I got pretty talkative as I piled on the stories about what it was like to be children in the Valley. Bo loved my telling about him. I enjoyed the company. Partly, I guess, because I was the center of attention and felt more clever than I really am.

After dinner we walked back to Bo's place. It's only about four blocks away from the restaurant.

Jo and I sat in the livingroom talking. Bo put on some tango music, nice and low so we didn't have to shout. Bo kept bringing out the pastries and putting them on the table. He brought in a bottle of white wine in a blue bottle, and Cokes, and a bottle of spiced rum, and Kahlua. He plugged in the coffee pot and started some coffee brewing. He had the caramel corn in a big bowl. I thought it was pretty keen.

Bo poured some of that chilled wine into glasses for Jo and himself. I fixed myself a strong rum and Coke. It was starting out to be a neat party.

Bo went back to his bedroom and came back to the livingroom with a bong and a couple of those mini-pipes that are designed for smoking dope. All three pipes were loaded with pot and there were a bunch of cut-up buds in a saucer close to the pipes. And, of course, several books of matches were out on the table.

"O.K., guys," Bo said. "The bong's to be shared by any bongers in the room…meaning, at least, me."

Jo and I applauded. I don't know why. It just seemed like the thing to do.

"For anyone who is not in a bong-sharing mood," Bo went on, "we have, for your smoking pleasure, these cute little pipes. Anyone who wants can grab one, and take it into a quiet corner and…suck."

Jo and I laughed and applauded again.

I picked up one of the little pipes. Bo lit the bong and took a hit. Jo took a hit from the bong right after him. I lit my little pipe and inhaled. I refilled my glass with rum and Coke, put a slice of that chocolaty-type cake on a plate, and headed for Bo's big overstuffed chair. I doubted he'd be using it, and the sidetable next to it was just right for accommodating my pipe, matches, drink, and cake.

The lights were low and Bo lit a few candles and several of those incense sticks he'd bought up at Haight.

Bo and Jo sat at the table and shared one of the French pastries and sipped some of that white wine out of the same wine glass.

I'd smoked marijuana before. Of course. Who hasn't? I'd never been real big on dope. Budweiser is my mood enhancer of choice. Followed by rum and Coke. But if grass is being smoked at a party, I don't mind sucking in a puff or two.

Down home, my buddy Boomer's a bachelor like me. He's a real sports nut, like Rat. Skeeter and I are fans, you know, but we weren't real jocks in high school. So we're big fans, but football, baseball and basketball aren't our whole lives, either.

Boomer has a TV screen fills a whole damn wall at his place. He has a satellite dish and can pick up a sporting event any time, anywhere in the world. He always has big dough riding on the games with his bookie Armen over in Visalia.

During football season all Boomer's buddies are at his place to watch the Sunday games and, of course, Monday night football. He has a great big ice chest out in the room. We bring our own beer cans or bottles and plop them in the chest. Everyone brings a dip or chips, or crackers, or finger food, and we all share while we watch the games. Skeeter and Rat show up when they can get away from their old ladies.

Once in a while our buddy Moe will bring some joints to Boomer's. None of us smoke much during the game. Quite a few of the guys don't smoke it at all. They just don't like it. Cool!

I'd never tried a bong before, or any kind of pipe, for that matter. But sitting in that big comfortable chair at Bo's, with the soft lights, the incense smell, the music, the rum, the cake, and all, I kind of got a kick out of lighting that little pipe from time to time and taking hit after hit.

I couldn't think of anything more amusing to do than watch Bo and Jo while I toked, and munched, and tippled. They each took another toke on the bong and then got up to dance. Bo led, Jo followed.

Those two dudes did a really mean tango. I got to shouting things like "Olé," and "Way to go," and "It takes two." I thought I was funny as Hell and the two guys didn't miss a beat because of my shenanigans.

I finished off that chunk of cake. *Really* good. And somehow I'd drunk all my rum and Coke. I got up to go to the table for refills and found I wasn't as steady on my feet as I thought I was. Jesus! How could Cousin Bo and his boyfriend dance so well when I was having trouble navigating.

I got back to the chair with a big bowl of caramel corn and my refreshed drink. What I found I also had picked up was a refill of pot for my pipe. Well, what do you know? I didn't even remember picking that sucker up.

I set the munchies and the drink on the table, emptied the ashes from the pipe, and stuffed in the fresh weed.

I sank into the chair and lit up. Suddenly, everything was funny as Hell. The crunch of the popcorn in my mouth made me giggle. The sweet drink bubbled down my throat giving me happy goosebumps. The two guys dancing were a goddam riot. I was chuckling to myself, and the guys were oblivious to my presence.

They would dance and toke. They would munch and dance. They would dance and drink. I stopped shouting my encouragement and just kept munching and giggling, drinking and laughing, toking and chortling.

God! Was I ever having a time for myself.

The two dudes took off their shirts and undershirts. They tangoed around gracefully, bare chested, the one with nearly transparent alabaster skin, the other California tanned. It was damned fascinating.

The CD came to its end. Bo put on a new one. It wasn't a tango album this time but waltzes. You know, the kind like the Blue Danube and all that? Kind of classical.

My God, how those two cut a rug, as my grandpa used to say. Bo led

Jo around the room, spinning around, twirling even. Beat the Hell out of me how they could do all that when I had trouble even getting out of my chair to get to the can. But I had to go, and to get there without the dancing boys running over me.

I made it to the john all right.

When I'd finished, I washed my hands and got back to the livingroom, kind of keeping time to the music with my feet.

Bo and Jo had taken their shoes off and were scarfing down some of that cake. The coffee had brewed a while back and they were drinking a cup of it laced with Kahlua. I could tell because the liqueur bottle was uncapped on the table right in front of them.

It sounded good. I poured myself a coffee, grabbed a couple of those French pastries and another little bud of maryjane, zapped a big shot of Kahlua into the java, went to my chair, and decided to take my shoes off, too, and get comfy.

The hot spiked coffee went down real good with those tasty pastries. I reloaded my pipe with the pot and took another little toke.

I focused my eyes on the two dudes. Sure, one of them was my cousin whom I'd known all my life. But, then again, he was someone else. He was a stranger, and interesting as all Hell, too. And I knew that super-white dude Jo as well as I knew Bo. Really. The two of them were kissing. Funniest thing I ever saw. Two dudes kissing one another. What do you think about that?

They had their hands all over each other, and next thing you know they took off for Bo's bedroom

Next thing I knew, sunshine was coming through the window, and I had to piss something awful.

I struggled up out of the chair, hit the can, got to my den and flopped down on my bed fully clothed.

It was late morning when I woke up again. I heard sounds of dishes clinking in the other room. The bathroom was clear.

I brushed my teeth, showered, shaved, and got into fresh clothes.

When I got to the livingroom Bo was sitting at the kitchen passthrough drinking coffee. Jo had obviously left sometime earlier. The room had been picked up. You'd never know there had been a party there the night before.

Bo poured me a cup. I sat on the stool next to him and sipped. We didn't say a word to each other.

And as I drank my coffee, I wondered about the world I had stepped into.

Later, Bo and I took a walk over to Castro Street to The Grind, a coffee house that's kind of a morning gathering place. But it was no longer really morning. There were plenty of other late risers there nursing their lattes like we were.

After the coffee at the apartment and the lattes at The Grind, Bo and I got to talking again. We didn't mention the previous night's party. I don't know why. We just never ever discussed it.

Bo said, "Doc, I have been derelict in my duty."

"Tell me about your duty, Bo."

"Yesterday I told you I had a surprise for you today."

"Yeah. You said something like you were going to find me a gal who wasn't jail bait."

"And who will give you an experience like you've never had before," he added.

"Not a cross dresser like Darlene though?" I asked with a raised eyebrow.

"No," he laughed. "Straight like you. I promise you a real, genuine, honest-to-God female."

"So," I asked. "What's so different about her that she'll be like nothing I've ever had before?"

"Her slit runs sideways," Bo said with a wink.

"You mean, instead of up and down…?"

"It goes from side to side."

I got it.

"You've lined me up a Chinese doll!"

"You've got it, Buddy Boy. We're off to Grant Avenue this afternoon."

"Grant Avenue?"

"That's Chinatown, My Friend."

"How do you fuck an Oriental?" I asked. "Crosswise? Like we make an X with our bodies while we're doing it or something?"

"How would *I* know?" Bo laughed. "You'll have to figure it out yourself. You're the one who's straight, not me."

Ever since I'd learned from the other guys in my class in grammar school that Chinese girls have their cunts going sideways instead of up and down, I'd wondered exactly how the Chinese get it on in bed. We guys used to discuss that a lot. There were always some wiseguys who said Chinese snatch runs up and down, not across. But none of those know-it-alls were part of our "in" group, so their opinions did not count.

Bo and I caught the bus up Market to Powell and walked from there. We went up Powell to Union Square and its shops. Then we cut across the Square to Stockton Street and took it up to Bush. A right turn took us to Grant Avenue and the Chinatown Gateway Arch.

I remembered that gate from back when I was about ten and my folks brought me to Frisco to ride the cablecars, go to Fisherman's Wharf, see the zoo and the aquarium, and then take in Chinatown. It was a long exhausting day, but I remember it as being fun. I hadn't been to the city since then, but I remembered that Chinese gate.

Bo and I wandered through a couple of those shops that sell Chinesey junk to tourists. A little of that goes a long way. We just kind of sauntered along, taking in the tourists as much as the Chinese. I hoped Bo and I didn't look like most of the goddam tourists. But I knew we couldn't pass for Chinese, either, so what did that leave?

It was a little late for lunch, but we hadn't had much to eat that morning so when we got up to Jackson Street Bo suggested we stop in for a bite of dim sum. I didn't know dim sum from dumb-dumb. I still don't. But I could use a bit of sustenance so we went into this place called Home of Dim Sum, just off Grant on Jackson. There were a bunch of steaming baskets in there containing God knows what. Bo ordered for us at the counter, and we took our food to a table. It was mostly different kinds of stuffed dumplings and then there was also stuff wrapped in leaves. I had a Coke with mine. Bo had tea.

It was really pretty good, and it was filling. Cheap, too.

After we finished that dim sum stuff, we headed eastward on Jackson past Ross Alley to Stockton Street. On Stockton there's a bar called Great Art's. We stepped inside.

It was your standard saloon with a bar and cocktail tables and chairs. The only thing different about it was that nearly everyone in the place was Oriental. I spotted four white dudes at a table quietly drinking cocktails. Everyone else I could see, though, was Asian.

"This is where we'll meet when we're both finished with what we'll be doing on Ross Alley," Bo said.

"What are we going to be doing on Ross Alley?" I asked.

"You're going to get laid. And I'm going to get stoned. Then, I'll see you here at Great Art's."

That sounded good to me. We went back out to Stockton Street, circled back to Jackson and then down Ross Alley.

It's not much of a street. It is narrow and unlike all the other streets we'd been on in Chinatown. It doesn't have any stores or restaurants on it. Just doors to what looked like kind of run down apartment buildings all along it.

"Back in the old days," Bo explained, "Ross Alley was where the Chinese whorehouses, gambling houses and opium dens were located. It was pretty wide open back in the Barbary Coast days. Now, as you see, it's not exactly bustling with people. But that doesn't mean the old trades aren't still carried on here. It's just that you have to know which door to find and how to get through it."

"And, I'll bet *you* know, Bo," I ventured.

"I've been around here before," he smiled.

The doors facing the alley all looked about the same to me. But the places do have street numbers. We stopped at a black door and Bo rang the bell.

A peep window opened and an Oriental looking eye appeared through it.

"Yes?"

"Nee how," Bo said.

"How bah," was the answer and the door opened just wide enough for us to sidle through.

The alleyway and the buildings along it had not been very impressive. But inside this building it was luxurious. We were in a large livingroom with Chinesey furnishings. The walls were pearl colored, the furniture was all black and white. There were large paintings on the walls, mainly of imposing looking Chinese mandarins or something.

The Chinese man who let us in was wearing a robe. On his head he had on one of those Chinese skull caps like they sell in the junk shops on Grant Avenue. He pointed to a low-lying table with a couple of kind of small chairs and motioned for us to sit down. Other than the greeting he'd given us through the peephole, he didn't say anything.

Bo reached in his pocket and took out a piece of paper with some Chinese writing on it and handed it to the dude. The guy inspected it carefully and grunted. Bo got a few hundred dollar bills out then and passed them to the guy, who studied them closely, too. Then he stuffed the note and the dough into his sleeve as we sat down.

Our silent host bowed slightly and shuffled out of the room.

I didn't say a thing. I just kind of took it all in. Bo seemed to know exactly what he was doing. So I just relaxed into the scene.

We sat there looking around and staring at each other for about five minutes. Nothing was happening. It was perfectly silent in that pearl-colored room. There wasn't so much as a tick of a clock to break the quiet.

Then in came a gorgeous Oriental girl carrying a tray. It's hard to describe her. She was wearing an embroidered gown. In her long, jet-black hair she had a white flower. Her skin was like soft peach color and had a subtle glow to it. She had the most beautiful features you can imagine, but it was her mouth that spelled perfection.

"Welcome to our humble home," she said as she placed her tray on the table. "My name is May Flower."

I nearly laughed. I thought that she didn't look like she'd come over on the Mayflower. More like on a celestial ship from Heaven. I was in love.

The babe poured Bo and me some fragrant tea in very small cups. Bo sipped his, and so did I.

Bo didn't say anything, so neither did I. I guess there's not too much chit chat in one of those places. I wasn't real sure exactly what kind of place this was, but whatever it was, I was ready to go with the flow.

The Chinese guy came back into the room while we were sipping our tea. He gave a little bow to Bo. Bo stood up. I started to get up, too, but Bo signaled me to stay seated and May Flower's soft delicate hands pressed gently on my shoulders as another signal that it wasn't my turn to get up.

"See you at Great Art's," Bo said to me in a low voice, almost a whisper. He followed the dude in the robe to the back of the room and the two of them disappeared around a corner.

When they were gone, May Flower gently ran her hands over my face in a caress, touched my lips in a way that sent shock waves throughout my body.

She said, "Follow me."

You'd better believe. I followed.

She took my hand in her small, thin, delicate one and led me to the end of the room. A turn down a hallway and we came to a flight of stairs. She led me up the steps and I followed eagerly.

On the second floor hallway there were three doors on either side. She led me through the center door on the left.

The room I found myself in was painted a very gentle, soothing shade of blue. The next thing I noticed was that there was a bubbling Jacuzzi sunk into the floor. To the right of the spa was a Western style bed and next to the bed was a little table with a bunch of jars on it. Nothing about that room appeared very oriental. All I knew was that I was going to get laid. And by the loveliest looking woman I had ever seen.

There was a chair next to the wall. She asked me to sit down and take off my shoes and socks. I did so, of course. There was a shoe rack next to the chair. I put my shoes on it very carefully, trying to appear very civilized.

She beckoned me to step up to where she was standing.

"Stand right there, very still, please," she ordered in about the softest, sweetest voice you can imagine.

I obeyed. Hell, if she'd asked me to stand on my head and sing the Star Spangled Banner I would have obeyed.

As I stood there, she removed my garments, very slowly, very methodically, giving loving rubs to my skin each time a piece of clothing slipped off.

In due time I was standing there facing her buck-ass naked, sporting a throbbing hardon.

Then, facing me, looking demure, she proceeded to take off her robe. There was nothing underneath that robe but an exquisite body. Her breasts were small and perfectly rounded.

I stared and stared at her. I had to see which way her koozie was oriented. North and South? I couldn't see. East and West? Hard to imagine. But I figured time would tell. Whichever way it ran, she was truly lovely. Bo was treating me to something *very* special.

She led me to the Jacuzzi. We entered the bubbling waters. They were somewhere between warm and hot. Good! I don't like it when the temperature's too hot. The water was somewhat scented. The smell wasn't too unlike the tea I'd had downstairs.

We sat down into the water.

After a nice soak, she led me over towards the bed.

She asked me to lie down on the bed. As I did so she hastily dried herself off.

What followed was like an oriental dream. There was nothing dirty, base, or nasty about it. All I can say is that it beat any experience I ever had before or since.

I finally got out of the bed, dressed myself and put my shoes and socks back on. As I was doing so, I said, "May Flower. I love you."

"Of course," she replied, smiling sweetly. "All you Round-eyes love me. I'm very good."

"Your damned tootin' you are," I agreed.

She opened the door for me and I followed her down the stairs into the pearl-colored livingroom. I wanted to kiss her goodbye, but she would have none of it.

When she quietly closed the door behind me I stood there in Ross Alley and wondered if what I'd gone through was actually real. Because I had been in another world. A world I liked a lot.

When I got to Great Art's Saloon on Stockton, Bo wasn't there yet. I sat at the bar and ordered a Bud. The barkeep was a Chinese guy who wasn't big on being sociable. O.K. by me. I had my reveries to keep me company.

I'd put down three Buds when Bo came waltzing into the bar. He ordered a kir, whatever the Hell that is, and we went to find a table. I carried my latest Bud with me.

"You know pretty much what I was doing," I told him. "How did you keep yourself busy?"

"There's a basement under that building," he told me. "That's where the opium parlor is."

"Opium 'parlor'?" I asked.

"The management there discourages the use of the word 'den.' What they have are some very stylish private rooms where you can stretch out in style and smoke your dope. It's not like in a Fu Manchu novel."

I'd never read a Fu Manchu novel, but I could guess how an opium den would be described in those kinds of books.

"It was real nice in there," Bo said. "Soft piped-in music. A few puffs and I was into the sweetest dreams imaginable. I can't describe the dreams. They'd just sound boring if I tried to tell you what I saw and felt."

I've always hated it when anyone tried to tell me about their stupid dreams anyway – opium or no opium.

He asked me abut my experience.

I thanked Cousin Bo heartily for the best sex I'd ever had. Then, as far as I was able to, I described what May Flower had done for me.

When I finished Bo exclaimed, "Christ Almighty. It's nearly enough to make me wish I was straight."

Bo asked me about what he called May Flower's pudenda. I understood what he meant – her twat. But I had to tell him the truth.

"I really don't know. At the time it really didn't make any difference. Whichever way it went, it was heaven."

Bo seemed to understand.

After that, we didn't have much to say to each other on our walk back down to Market Street or on the bus. We didn't need to. We'd each had ourselves a time.

It was several days until the weekend and Bo and I didn't do much in the way of going out and partying. But on Thursday he asked me if I'd like to take in one of the girlie shows in North Beach on Friday night. I didn't know what North Beach was, but girlie show sounded good. The answer was "yes."

Bo explained to me that there isn't any beach at North Beach any more. But that back in the sailing ship era, the area was called the Barbary Coast. That didn't ring any bells with me either, but I didn't want to say so.

After it stopped being called the Barbary Coast it became an Italian neighborhood. Later it was where the Beatniks hung out.

I knew what an Italian is. But Beatnik? Beats me. Probably some kind of gay thing.

What Bo was leading up to was that North Beach was where the Condor Club had been back in the sixties. Carol Doda was a dancer on stage there and she was the first broad to dance baring her breasts all the way. That was in 1964.

So? Big deal.

Then this Carol dame went on to take it all off. Topless and bottomless. That was the first club in the world where that had happened according to Bo.

I doubted that. But far be it from me to pour cold water on my cousin's boring history lesson. I waited for more.

"The Condor Club's been closed now for years," Bo said. "But even though topless and bottomless shows are no big deal any more, people like to go to North Beach still to see the shows. And the most famous ecdysiast today is Flaming Mame."

Ecdysiast? I figured that must mean stripper.

"Mame does her act just about a block away from where the old Condor Club used to be. Her place is on Romolo Court. I thought you might like to take it in."

A nudie show? It sounded like good innocent fun. But I was puzzled. It didn't sound like Bo's kind of thing at all. So I asked him.

"You're right," he said. "What I thought I'd do is drop you off at

Flaming Mame's Club and I'd go on up a few blocks to Green Street where there's a theater called the Boylesque that has a show with male strippers. The Boylesque draws curious females who whistle and shout when the guys on stage get to dancing with their peters flipping in the breeze. And we gay males just sit there and enjoy seeing those gorgeous dongs jiggling and flipping around. I'll be well entertained while you're ogling Mame. Okay?"

It sounded to me like good Friday night entertainment for both of us.

Friday evening we drove to Portsmouth Square. There's a parking garage under the square.

The Square is shared by three major Frisco neighborhoods, Chinatown, the Financial District, and North Beach. Bo had checked out that the shows at Flaming Mame's and at the Boylesque both started at eight o'clock. So we got to Portsmouth Square about six-thirty so we could get in some dinner before our shows.

After we'd parked, we hotfooted it up to the Black Cat Restaurant at Broadway and Kearny. It was definitely Bo's kind of place. It's done in what Bo calls art deco. The menu is kind of French and hard to read. The diners seemed about as gay to me as the folks in the Castro.

I let Bo order for me and the food really was very good and the people-watching was as good as it gets anywhere I'd been in Frisco.

When we finished eating we walked over to the Tosca Bar on Columbus Avenue. It's more than just a bar. It specializes in "real" cappuccinos, which seems to mean coffee with brandy in it. We each had one of those.

"After each of us has seen his show, we'll come back here to meet," Bo said. "No telling whether our shows will let out at the same time, so this is as good a place to hang out as any while we wait for each other."

Sounded good to me. I saw that they serve Bud. No problem.

After our coffees, we trotted up to Broadway and to Flaming Mame's. Bo left me at the entry door and went on up Columbus to where his Boylesque show was.

I thought Flaming Mame's place looked kind of ratty. But then, maybe that's part of the idea. It was supposed to be kind of retro sixties, so ratty might be what your ordinary tourist's looking for.

The goon at the door warned me that the cover was fifty bucks and that there was a two drink minimum on top of that. Since they struck oil at my place, I wouldn't have flinched if the cover was three or four times that. And I intended to have more than two brews anyway.

Inside, there was a stage at the far end with a curtain and an orchestra pit in front. The cabaret tables were little round jobbies. I slipped the usher-type chick fifty bucks and she sat me front-center, practically in the pit. The five piece band was already playing these old songs from way before my time. It was all right, but I was wondering if I was going to like a couple of hours of this so-called entertainment. I ordered six Buds.

"I'm sorry," a sleazy looking waiter said. "We don't serve Budweiser."

"What do you serve?" I asked.

"Michelob and Coors Lite."

Jesus! No Bud. Well, Michelob would do.

"Bring me six bottles of the damned Michelob, then," I ordered. I figured I'd better get myself in a good mood. Things weren't looking too nifty at that point.

The sleezebucket waiter brought me my brews. I didn't like the way he smiled at me. Kind of like he thought I was a hick from the sticks and he was Mister Big Shot. Know what I mean?

The customers kept coming in, and by showtime at eight the place was packed and noisy. And it could have used a little air conditioning. It was hot and stuffy and kind of smelly.

The band struck up an overture, the curtain went up, and there were twenty dancing girls on stage in skimpy outfits. They pranced around to the music, wiggled their asses, and it wasn't too bad. At the end of their routine they snapped off their bras and jiggled their hooters. The audience liked it and clapped, hooted, and hollered.

In the next act, the gals were topless when the curtain went up. They jiggled around some more, and at the end of the routine they shed their g-strings, so they were topless and bottomless. Tits and bush flashing at us. It was O.K., but I'd seen as much at the Apollo Theater over in the Valley, up in Sacramento.

The band played a flourish and the gals came down the steps at the end of the stage and into the audience. They had sparkling yo-yos, and walked among the tables playing with those ridiculous yo-yos. Kind of amusing but no big thing.

A comedian came out on stage. The chicks settled down at the tables with the customers.

One of the dancing girls, kind of pretty, well-stacked, asked me if she could sit at my table while the comic was doing his routine.

At the nudie clubs down in the Valley I'd had the girls at my table. You buy them a couple of watered down drinks, they keep their breasts pointing at you, you get a good eyeful, and that's it. Same here at this place. Look, but don't touch.

I bought this chick who'd just sat at my table a glass of twenty-five dollar "champagne." We couldn't really talk because the comedian was yakking all the time.

I saw that this was a clipjoint, just like any other. Milk the rubes for all you can. Flash them a little forbidden view from time to time and see how much they'll spend.

I'd had enough beers that I was mellow, though. And what the Hell! I was ready now to relax and just enjoy the girlies. I didn't expect too much then. Let the good times roll, huh?

The sleazebucket kept the overpriced brews coming and I kept downing them with regular trips to the john to download the used beer. I got mellower and mellower.

When the dancing girls had done a few numbers and had paid three visits to us chumps at the tables, it was time for the main act.

Ho hum. It was going to be a solo act displaying more flesh. I'd taken in enough female anatomy by then that the broad had better be good. But frankly, I wasn't expecting much.

The band struck up some goddam sixties number. Something I'd heard before on a real oldies program but I couldn't tell you what it was called.

And out came Flaming Mame.

Good God Almighty! Forget about May Flower. Forget about every chick I'd ever known. I was in LOVE!

Mame had on a wisp of a bra, a g-string and high heeled shoes. But my amazed eyes didn't know where to fix themselves. Her hooters were real jugs. Big and round, with cleavage you could dive into and never come out. Legs that were so perfect you wanted to climb up them forever and go to sleep. Ass? So round, so firm, so downright kissable. Face? That of a paper doll! And her hair. Lots and lots of hair. And flame red. You would have thought her head was on fire. This was the woman of my dreams. And I didn't think it was just the Michelob shouting at me.

All that, and she could sing and dance, too.

She was doing some lively footwork to that old-time music, her parts bouncing here, there, and everywhere.

With the music still playing, she came down the steps and into the audience. She came dancing down the front row, where I was staked out. When she was right in front of my table she flipped her bra off. The crowd went wild. I like to fainted. My pecker stood up in my pants and saluted.

She leaned over my table, winked at me, and said, "How you doing, Big Boy?" I gulped, "Fine." Then she winked at me again and moved on down a couple of tables. I think she'd spotted the tenting in my pants.

She went sashaying all around the cabaret, but I could tell she wasn't giving any of the other customers what she'd given me. It seemed she really liked me.

At intermission I had to go to the john. I'd downed lots and lots of beer.

When I got back to my table the sleazebucket waiter was loading my table with a couple more beers.

"Hey," I said, waving a twenty dollar bill in the air. "Is there any way I can get backstage and meet Mame?"

He took the twenty bucks in a snap.

"Can't be done, Boss," he replied. "Strictly no civilians allowed backstage. City ordinance. We'd get shut down. But see me after the show's over. If you're a big spender, I can maybe help you. I noticed Mame had eyes for you, Mister. But you've got to know. She's only interested in big spenders."

He went on about his business. But he had me real excited. "Big spender?" Sure, that was me. And he'd noticed how she had eyes for me. Hot damn! I was sure I had sweeter dreams, sitting there wide awake ogling Mame, than Bo had over at the opium den on Ross Alley a few days back.

I could hardly wait for the second act. The chicks came on first again. When the babe I'd bought the "champagne" for before came back to my table I bought her another couple of the over-priced bubbly wines and then openly gave her a fifty dollar tip. I had to show I was an obvious big spender.

After the crummy acts that followed had run their course, it was Flaming Mame's turn to come out onto the stage again. Out she trounced onto the stage, topless this time. She sang and danced and bounced and got me all hot and bothered. Then, just when I knew it was going to happen, she shed the Goddam g-string.

And there she was. She was completely nude. Jesus! I was ecstatic!

The house went wild. I was shouting and laughing and clapping and whistling like the rest of them. I could swear Mame looked right at me and winked. But I couldn't really be sure because I was so engrossed devouring her tits and cunt with my eyes.

That was the end of the act, and the end of the show. The sleazebag came around with my bill.

"Wait around," he said. "I'll get back to you when I've picked up everyone else's tabs."

Oh, I'd wait all right.

My own tab, for cover, beers, drinks for the chick, and all was over three hundred bucks. How can *anyone* drink three hundred dollars worth of beer, even with cover and chick's drinks included? I'll tell you someone who can. Mister Big Spender, that's who.

I put my tab on my credit card. When the sleaze came back with the slip for me to sign, he saw that I'd left him a healthy tip. Big spender!

"Well," I said. "How do I get to meet Mame?"

"She says I can give you her home address."

"Good," I enthused. "Give it to me."

"She has to know you're sincere."

"Meaning?"

"It'll cost you five hundred. Cash. No checks or credit cards. You don't carry around that kind of dough, come back some other time."

I had five C-notes on me, of course. And plenty to spare. I laid the five bills in his outstretched hand.

"That's just for her," he sneered. "I'm supposed to get a tip for my trouble."

Bastard! I'd overtipped him already for the tab. But what the Hell. No time to stop being Mister Big Spender. I topped off the pile with a fifty.

"Here," he said, handing me a piece of paper. "This is her address. When you get there, the moves are up to you. I don't make any guarantees. And one more thing. You see Mame up there on the stage or down here on the floor, she's all made up. The red hair – it's a wig. The way she looks, it's entirely different when she's out of the theater and at home. So don't be shocked by what you see. Okay?"

Sure, sure, sure. I didn't just fall off the turnip truck. I knew she wasn't a whore, so I'd have to make points with her. Take her out and show her a big time by spending money like a son of a bitch. And I knew all dames look different without their makeup. Shit, I was in love with that babe. I'd take her as I found her and win her heart by spreading my dough wherever she wanted to go and do with her whatever she wanted to do.

Written on the paper was the address I'd paid for. It was on Powell Street. Heck, I knew where that was. I'd walked up Powell. I could get there from Bo's on the bus. And if I didn't feel like walking, the cable car runs right up that hill that Powell's on.

I got to hankering for tomorrow. I was going to go visit the love of my life.

I whistled all the way back to that Tosca Bar. Bo was already there, drinking that coffee thing. I ordered a Bud.

"So," I asked him. "How did it go?"

"They've got some real hot studs there at the Boylesque," Bo said. "They can tease the ladies and they are real eye candy for me and my kind. It was great. How about you?" I told him I had the address of the hottest woman I'd ever seen. He didn't ask me how I got it. I didn't tell him.

We drove back to the Castro two happy dudes.

VOICE OF MAMIE APFELSTIRN

I came here to San Francisco from Calaveras County. That's up in the High Sierras, you know.

My daddy, Reverend Amos Apfelstirn, was a preacher who went to the mining camps up there to save souls. Momma took along a portable footpedal organ and played the hymns. I used to be the whole choir and tried to lead the mining and lumbering boys in the hymns.

Daddy and Momma named me Mamie, after a first lady they admired. So, that's me. Mamie Apfelstirn, preacher's daughter.

My folks were awful strict. Those mountain boys up there in Calaveras can be mighty wild. So my parents protected me something fierce. I wasn't allowed to go anywhere without a chaperone. Never had a boyfriend. Never really knew anything about S-E-X. If you know what I mean.

There was a big tragedy in my life a couple of years ago. It was midwinter. Daddy and Momma took off early Sunday morning for Darrington to do a service. They left me behind that day because I had a bad case of the flu and had to stay in bed.

They never got to Darrington. An avalanche crashed down on the road on their way there and killed them outright.

Miners and loggers from all over the county took up a collection for me at the funeral. Those are very generous people. I had more money than I'd ever seen in my whole life.

What I decided to do with the money was leave Calaveras County, come down here to San Francisco, and see what life was all about.

I took a secretarial class here in town, and found out I was very good at typing and stenotyping. I got a job real easy down on Montgomery in the financial district. And I was taking very good care of myself moneywise.

Talking to the other girls at the office, I heard a lot of things I'd never heard at all up there in the mountains. One important thing I learned, I figured out for myself. I was the only twenty-two year old virgin in San Francisco. The only problem was, I didn't really know exactly what that meant.

If I was going to be a city girl, I had to learn about sex. But I was so inexperienced I didn't know where to begin.

So I looked through the yellow pages of the telephone book. And I found a heading SEX THERAPISTS.

That's what I needed. A professional.

I called the number and got a receptionist. I told her I wanted to make an appointment. She asked me if I wanted to come to the office or have the doctor make a housecall.

I told her I'd be embarrassed to go to an office that said "sex therapist" on the door. She said a lot of people felt that way. That's why there was a housecall option.

I gave her my name and my address here on Powell Street.

The receptionist said they would get back to me when one of the therapists had an opening.

I was waiting to hear back from them when, one day, to my surprise, my doorbell rang. I just *knew* it was the sex therapist coming to teach me how to overcome being the only twenty-two year old virgin in this big city.

VOICE OF DOC KINKAID

I woke up the next morning thinking of nothing but Flaming Mame. I thought about her as I brushed my teeth, showered and shaved. I was going to see the woman of my dreams that morning. Poor Bo had to put up with my smiling and simpering all through breakfast. I'll bet he was happy to have me get my cheerful face out the door and be off on my way to my date with destiny.

I caught the bus on Broadway and got off at Powell. I didn't know how the numbers ran, so I had to figure that out first.

Once I'd got the feel for the addresses the question was whether to catch a cable car or trudge up the hill. I was in such high spirits I decided to hoof it.

When I got to the address on that piece of paper that I'd carried next to my heart I saw that Mame lived in a nice apartment building. There was a callbox and I pushed the button for the apartment I wanted.

"Hello?" came the answer.

"Hello, Mame? It's Doc. Can you let me in?"

"Oh, Doctor," she said. "Come in. I wasn't expecting you so soon."

A buzzer sounded at the door. I pushed it open and entered the lobby. The apartment number was on the third floor. There was an elevator but I took the stairs. I just could hardly control my energy.

When I got to her door I rang the bell. She opened the door immediately.

"Come in, Doctor," she said.

The sleazebucket had told me she would look different. Boy, was he ever right. Of course I knew the red wig would be off. She had kind of short light brown hair. It wasn't that that was surprising. Her face was a different shape. Her breasts must have been tightly compressed by a bra because they were not humungous like when she performed. And she was…well…just completely different. But I definitely liked what I saw. I decided on the spot that I really liked the way she looked offstage even better than the appearance she put on at the club. I was pleased.

"Won't you sit down, Doctor?" she invited.

I sat on the sofa. She sat in a chair.

"Well, first off, Mame, I'd rather you called me Doc instead of Doctor. 'Doctor' really isn't what anyone calls me."

"I understand," she answered. "Considering what this is all about, it's probably best to be somewhat informal. And, also, my name's really Mamie, not Mame."

I got it. Mame was her stage name. It worked with "Flaming." I liked the sound of Mamie better. It fit this neat chick when she wasn't performing.

"First off," Mamie said. "I think we ought to discuss money. What are the rates?"

Rates? I was brand new at this sort of thing and couldn't make sense of "rates."

"Money is no object," I said. "I'm loaded. You don't have to worry. I really *am* a big spender."

She looked very puzzled. I didn't know why because I'd made it clear to the sleazebucket that I was Mister Big Spender and supposedly he'd told her.

There was a long awkward pause. Neither of us seemed to know what to say next. At last she said, "We both know why you're here. I suppose we should get started."

I thought that was a great idea.

"Terrific," I replied. "I think so, too."

"Well," she said. "To begin with, I guess you know I'm a virgin."

That surprised the Hell out of me.

"I never would have guessed," I said. "That's absolutely amazing."

"All the girls I work with would think so too, if they knew. I figured out that I am probably the only twenty-two year old virgin in San Francisco."

"That is probably true," I marveled.

"That's why I was so anxious for you to come by, Doctor…I mean Doc. I was hoping you could help me."

Boy, was I ever ready to be of assistance.

"I'll certainly try my best, Mame…Mamie."

"I don't know anything about all this," she admitted. "How do we begin?"

I suggested that some nice music in the background might be a good starting place.

We went together to the radio, fooled around with the dial, and found KSAF, the oldies station.

"I guess you like the oldies best, don't you?" I asked.

The gal singing on the radio was warbling something about "old black magic." I told Mamie I thought that would be a good background and we went back and sat down.

"Is there any way you'd like us to begin?" I asked.

"Yes, Doc. I've been giving a little thought to this. I'm having a lot of trouble about the vocabulary. Could we start there?"

Vocabulary? We had some nice retro music going. She claims she's a virgin and wants me to help her. And she wants a vocabulary lesson? Well, whatever she wanted was what I wished to give her. Because *this* was the real woman of my dreams. Better than May Flower. Better than the Flaming Mame of the stage. This Mamie who claims to be a virgin. She had to be kidding me about that. But whatever she wanted to pretend, I was willing to play her game. Because this time I was *really* in love.

"All right," I said. "Let's start with the vocabulary. I guess there are some words you're interested in. What are they?"

"You say some sex words," she answered, "and I'll see if I can guess what they mean."

"It's a game," I thought. "Isn't that cute? She wants to play a game of dirty words. Well, why not?"

So I thought I'd try out one of the tamer words meaning breast and see where it led. This could be fun. Not at all what I thought we'd be doing, but if that's what she wanted to play, I was ready to go for it.

"Here's a word," I said. "How about the word 'hooter'?"

"Oh, yes," she answered enthusiastically. "That's one I hear all the time at the office. What does it mean?"

"Office," I think. "Office? Wait a minute here. Just one little minute.

Flaming Mame doesn't work in an office. Apparently Mamie does. This is *not* Flaming Mame."

What a revelation! I'd been hornswaggled by the sleazebucket. He figured me for a rube and swindled me out of big bucks and then he'd written down some crazy address at random. The bastard.

But wait! Was this something to get upset about? The guy was a jerk all right. But look how it was turning out. His scam brought me to the woman of my dreams. Oh, boy! Now, I didn't want to mess my good fortune up. This was a gal who was pretty innocent and who was yearning to learn about what it's all about. And I was just the dude to teach her.

We started with that little vocabulary word. And I went on to teach her lots of the words we use here in the real world.

When she'd learned the basics, I thought maybe we should get some action going.

"Next," I said. "We should go into your bedroom. Is that all right with you?"

It was fine with her and we went directly to her boudoir.

"Now what?" she asked.

"We have to take our clothes off."

"Isn't that embarrassing?" she asked.

"You can get used to it, believe me," I told her. "It's all part of the vocabulary lesson."

"All right," she agreed.

We undressed.

I didn't have to explain what to do. I just led her through the motions.

"Will you marry me?" I asked after we'd done what needed to be done to free her from the awful fate of being a virgin. "If we were married, we could do this every day."

"I would like that very much," Mamie said.

We kissed and returned to our routine.

Mamie and I are married now. We live in her place here on Powell. I've revised my ideas about marriage completely. Maybe Skeeter and Rat were just married to the wrong kind of broads. Marriage with Mamie is a dream.

We're spending my money doing this city like it's never been done before. The only place I don't take her is Flaming Mame's. I don't know why. That just doesn't feel like too cool an idea.

I still have some things to teach Mrs. Mamie Kinkaid. But you'd be surprised what a fast learner she is.

PART FIVE

SCORING WITH FLAMING MAME

SCORING WITH FLAMING MAME

Harold Clump was in San Francisco at the California State Latin Teachers' Convention. At least that is what he told his wife. But his wife was down in Dulzura, at the bottom end of the state. And he was up in the Bay Area where she could not know what he was actually up to.

When Harold was out of the sight of his wife and beyond the bounds of his community, he pursued a special hobby. He loved to study the rites of Terpsichore. He reveled in the observances of Rajanata. He sought out the temples of the ecdysiasts. Or, to put it more simply, he very much enjoyed seeing women dance nude. Those jiggling breasts, those scrumptious legs, those forms divine.

Every year he managed to convince his wife that the California State Latin Teachers Association had invited him to deliver a paper at its annual convention in some far-away city, on some learned branch of the study of Latin literature. As it happened, the far-away city was always in a metropolis replete with theaters and clubs that feature exotic dancers. As the poet Virgil sang, "Sic itur ad astra."

On this particular trip to "deliver his paper," he had visited nudie clubs not only in San Francisco itself, but also down the peninsula in such sinful hamlets as Palo Alto and San Jose and across the Bay in Oakland and Berkeley. Oh, there was sin aplenty, far and wide.

One evening he went to a theater named for its featured terpsichorist, Flaming Mame. As always, he entered the theater wearing his signature trench coat and he did not remove that coat during the performance.

Before the show began, Harold sat at his little table sipping his glass of Chardonnay. He overheard two of the customers who appeared to be regulars at the show. One of the aficionados was saying to the other, "Hey, Dude. Did you hear that Mame lost Fido?"

His friend asked, "Is Fido her pet?"

The first man replied, "Her pet? It's that doggipin her latest squeeze gave her."

With the noise of the audience mounting, Harold could not hear more. But he did not need to.

Doggipin? What in the world is a "doggipin?" If it's called "Fido" it must be a breed of dog.

It was suddenly clear to him that the lead dancer in the show had lost a doggipin. Would it not be a lark if he, Harold Clump, could trace down the lost canine, retrieve it, and return it to the ecdysiast?

He was thinking of that when Flaming Mame appeared on stage. He sat at his little table in the back row, smiling merrily, as Mame's breasts, flipping about up on stage, held him entranced.

As Mame danced her erotic routine, Harold was doing a little routine of his own. He always accompanied nudie dancers with a little routine of his own beneath his trench coat.

He always arrived at nudie cabarets with his fly unbuttoned. At the first quivers of an erection his fist encircled his member and kept merry time to the music.

Over the years of following his hobby he had observed that many fellow audience members also accompanied the rhythms of the dance with vibrations under their trench coats. The correct name for the exercise, he of course knew, was 'onanism.' The vulgar called it jacking off.

When the curtain closed, a waitress approached his table. As chance would have it, she was one of his ex-students from Dulzura, Vanessa by name. She had come to San Francisco a few years previous and was supporting herself as a waitress at Flaming Mame's cabaret.

Vanessa recognized her old Latin teacher and was touched seeing him sitting at a table at the club where she worked. She thought it was cute that the professor enjoyed exotic dancing.

She had observed his masturbatory actions and was not shocked. She felt touched by her old teacher's loneliness.

She considered offering him a Kleenex, but thought better of it.

She politely waited until there was a break in the show.

"Ave, Grammatice," she greeted him in Latin. "Salve ad Flaming Mame's."

Harold recognized Vanessa at once. She had been an apt student and had really appeared to enjoy the intricacies of the Roman tongue. His erection had subsided and he stood to greet her.

"Ave, Vanessa," he said. And in a joking tone he asked, "What is a nice girl like you doing in a place like this?"

Vanessa explained that waitressing was her night job. She was attending the University of San Francisco studying to be a teacher.

"A Latin teacher by any chance?" Harold asked.

Vanessa was aware that there are more teaching jobs available in elementary schools than for teachers of classical languages in high schools. She explained, though, that she still loved Latin and had kept her old textbooks and occasionally read some Caesar, Cicero, or Virgil. Her former teacher was pleased to hear that.

"I've got to get back to work," she told him. "But is there anything I can do for you now?"

Harold had brought his own Kleenex, so didn't need that to wipe the excess jism from his fist. But he thought there was some slight possibility that Vanessa might, indeed, be able to give him a piece of esoteric information.

"Yes, Vanessa," he ventured. "Would you happen to know where Ms. Flaming Mame lives?"

"Why yes, Professor, I do," his former student replied. "My boyfriend drives taxi here in the city. He drove her home once. She lives at Eighty-seven Hobson Court."

That was exquisite news.

"Do you happen to know her apartment number?" he asked.

"No, Mr. Clump. I don't. But I *do* happen to know that her last name is Kuwak. That might help."

"Do you know how that's spelled?" Clump asked.

"Gee, no," she said. "Sorry. Have a good time while you're here in San Francisco."

And Vanessa returned to her job of picking up glasses and bottles from the tables. And Professor Clump returned to jacking off.

On his way back to his hotel that evening Harold walked past an all-night convenience store. He was inspired by an idea. Perhaps the way to catch a doggipin was with a hot dog.

He entered the store. In a freezer cabinet he found a frozen hot dog. The purchaser of the treat could, of course, heat it in the microwave and walk out with an instant treat. But there was no need for Harold to microwave the find for his purposes. It would be thawed by morning when he would need it. There was a display of plastic baskets along one of the aisles. He picked one up. It would be just the thing.

He left the store armed for the next morning's safari.

The next morning, after breakfast at the hotel's coffee shop, Harold was off to scour the seven hills of San Francisco in search of the doggipin. He had his thawed hot dog and the basket. One of the hotel's towels now lined his basket.

Up one twisty street and down another he drove. Harold was impressed that San Francisco, like Rome and Constantinople, is renowned for its seven hills. He drove up, over, and through all seven: Nob Hill, Russian Hill, Twin Peaks (which count as two), Mt. Sutro, Mt. Davidson, and Telegraph Hill. His eyes searched every sidewalk, every side street, every alleyway. No doggipins in sight. But intrepid hunter that he was, he was strong of heart and not discouraged. His weapon (hot dog wienie), and his trap (plastic basket) were resting in readiness on the passenger seat.

He had saved Telegraph Hill for last. Hobson Court is at the foot of that hill and was the most likely spot where Flaming Mame and her friends would have already diligently searched. And thus, by dialectic and inference, it was the least likely place to come upon the doggipin. But the mighty stalker would not be faint-hearted on his trek. If he had to mount the seven hills seven times, he would persevere.

But soft! One third of the way up Telegraph Hill what did Professor Harold Clump spy? His heart raced. His nostrils flared. There was a little white dog relieving himself on the sidewalk. It *had* to be a doggipin.

Harold parked very quietly. Armed with wienie and basket he stealthily approached the pooch. It had finished its job and was joyfully sniffing at the results of its efforts.

Harold held out the wienie.

"Here, Fido, here Fido," he called.

The beast faced him, saw the extended sausage, and could smell its aroma even above the delightful odor of its own leavings.

Harold was delighted. The dog apparently responded to the name "Fido." He was sure he had come upon the doggipin.

The animal came right up to the proffered delicacy. As it sniffed, Harold drew the morsel back over the edge of the basket.

Fido, for Harold was now sure that was the doggipin's name, followed the lure right into the trap. Once he was in, Harold let Fido begin munching down the rest of the hot dog. He covered the dog with the towel and carried dog-in-basket to the car.

The doggipin seemed to have taken a liking to the basket because it was quite content to remain in it and chew the treat the nice man had given him.

Hobson Court is not more than a ten minute drive down the hill. Harold, flushed with success, drove there with dog-in-basket and high hopes.

There was a parking space in front of 87 Hobson Court. "Omen faustum," Harold thought. It was a very good sign.

He got out of the car and removed the dog-enclosing basket. Fido had fallen contentedly asleep in his nest.

There was the customary callbox at the external door of the apartment building.

K-U-W-A-K. That was the name. Doctor Dillon Kuwak, D.N.A.T. Apartment 7. *Pro virtute felix temeritas*, right?

Harold rang the bell.

"Yes, what is it?" a male voice rasped.

"Package for Ms Kuwak," Harold answered.

At the sound of the buzzer Harold entered with his basketful of dog. Apartment seven was easy enough to find. The door to the apartment was open to the corridor and a bald, elderly gentleman in tiny glasses was peering out.

"Come in, come in," the gentleman urged.

Harold entered.

"Put the package there in the corner," the elderly personage ordered.

"Doctor Kuwak?" Harold inquired.

"Sit down, sit down," he was told. "You mustn't tire yourself."

Harold took a seat. His host sat in front of him and looked at him from head to foot.

"My name is Harold Clump," the visitor explained.

"And as you know," he was answered, "I am Doctor Dillon Kuwak, D.N.A.T. That is Doctor of New Age Therapies. And I can see that you got here just in time. You are in a parlous condition."

"I am?" Harold said with some concern.

"I can usually tell a person's condition at a glance," the doctor said. "But when someone like you comes to the door, I have to ask for a twenty dollar retainer."

Harold hesitated.

"Up front!" Doctor Kuwak insisted.

Harold was mystified, but reached in his wallet and extracted a twenty dollar bill. The doctor quickly pocketed the money and looked intently at Harold.

"Did you know your neck is flushed?" the doctor asked.

"No," Horace answered honestly. "I can't see my neck from here."

"And you have a small pimple on your left cheek."

Harold had noticed the pimple that morning while shaving and acknowledged so to the old guy.

"If you were a teenager, I wouldn't be overly concerned," Doctor Kuwak explained. "Adolescence causes pimples, you know. And sometimes flushed neck, too. But you're too old for that. So that leaves us with two possibilities as to what's wrong with you."

"Wrong with me?" Harold stammered.

The doctor told him one possibility was hemorrhoids.

"Hemorrhoids?" Harold exclaimed. "Where?"

"On your rectum," the doctor said.

Harold was comforted. He was afraid that he might have had hemorrhoids on his left cheek. That would be awful.

He assured Dr. Kuwak he had no piles on his rectum.

"That leads us to the second possibility," the doctor said. "Something much graver than hemorrhoids."

Harold wondered what could be worse than piles. He'd had them once and they were a pain in the…well, a pain.

"What have I got?" he asked.

"A too tight fitting prepuce," Dr. Kuwak diagnosed gravely.

*A tight foreskin? I'd never noticed **that** before.*

"I don't think so," he said.

"Are you, by any chance, Jewish?" Kuwak asked.

Harold assured him he was actually agnostic.

"Then that probably accounts for the flushed neck and the pimple," he was told.

"I need to examine your penis to verify my diagnosis," the good doctor explained. "Kindly unzip your fly and let me proceed with my examination."

Harold was flabbergasted. Unzip his fly?

But if that's what it took to meet Flaming Mame, he was game.

So he stood up and unzipped.

He shuddered involuntarily when the doctor reached in and carefully extracted the organ to be examined. The shaking continued as Dr. Kuwak skinned back the foreskin and said, "Hmmm. Tut-tut. You may pull that thing back into your trousers."

When Harold retrieved his penis and zipped, his trembling ceased. He sat back down.

"Yes," the doctor told him. "You decidedly are not Jewish."

"No," Harold replied. "I really am an agnostic."

"And what's more," Kuwak continued. "Your problem definitely is a too snug prepuce."

Harold wondered why being agnostic would be reason for him to have a flushed neck and a pimple on the cheek. The medical profession apparently was full of arcane surprises.

"I have just the remedy for you," the doctor said.

He went to a locked cabinet, unlocked it, brought out a jar, and then relocked the cabinet. He handed the jar to Horace.

"Here you are. Aloe vera mixed with motherwort. Just massage this on your glans penis."

Harold was pleased to hear a bit of Latin. It somehow soothed him.

"When should I apply it to my glans penis?" Harold asked.

"Just as soon as you have a little privacy. And as often as possible," he was told. "I think the case may be urgent. Now that will be twenty dollars."

Harold gave the doctor a twenty dollar bill for the medicine.

"You can go now," Kuwak told Harold. "Don't forget to take your medicine."

"This *is* where Ms Flaming Mame lives, isn't it?" Harold asked, trying to get back to why he had come there in the first place.

"Yes it is," he was answered.

"I take it that you are her father? Or perhaps her grandfather?" Harold inquired.

"No, I certainly am not," he was told. "I am her husband."

"Oh," Harold said in a rather apologetic tone.

"I'll tell you how it happened," Kuwak confided. "A while back, Miss Mame was feeling poorly. She had heard of my fame as a healer and came to my clinic here. I immediately diagnosed her as having an acute case of mimsy pip. I administered a potion of bladderwrack and fenugreek. Miracle cure, Sir.

A veritable miracle. That very evening she was back at her club singing and dancing up a storm."

"That's amazing," Harold said dubiously.

"The dear lady was so grateful," the doctor continued, "that two weeks later we went to Reno and got married."

Harold thought that was remarkable gratitude on her part.

"And five months later, Sir, I became a proud father. My lovely wife bore me a perfectly healthy bouncing baby boy."

Harold acknowledged that was indeed amazing.

"A very rare case, medically," Doctor Kuwak told him. "I was inclined to present the case to the San Francisco Medical Journal. But Mame, bless her heart, demurred. Like me, she eschews conventional medical practice. So I desisted."

"I understand completely," Harold agreed. "As Suetonius said, "Illud omnem fidem excedit.""

"Isn't that the truth," Kuwak agreed.

"Might I meet Mrs. Kuwak?" Harold asked, pursuing his original reason for coming to this clinic.

"Of course, Sir. She is always interested in meeting my patients. It may take a little while. So please be patient."

The doctor disappeared into the next room.

After a few minutes, Mame entered the room. She was wearing only a loose bra, a g-string, and a pair of high heels.

She greeted her guest with a lovely big smile.

"I brought you something," Harold stammered.

"Oh, how kind of you, Mister…"

"Clump," Harold said. "Harold Clump."

He rapidly wanted to get into the subject that had brought him there.

"What I brought you is a dog," Harold beamed.

"A dog!" Mame exclaimed. "What the Hell do *I* want with a goddam dog?"

Doctor Kuwak re-entered the room.

"Would you get a load of this, Dillon?" she laughed. "Mister Harold Clump brought me a goddam dog."

The two of them roared with laughter.

Harold pointed to the basket in the corner.

"It's Fido," he said. "The doggie you lost. I thought you would like him back."

That caused the couple to burst out anew with laughter.

"Oh," Kuwak exclaimed. "You thought Fido was a dog. That's a good one."

Harold was surprised to hear that Fido was not a dog at all.

Mame said, "Of course not. I can't stand pets. Fido is the name I gave to a diamond and ruby brooch, in the form of a dog's head. It was given to me by my very dear…"

She seemed to be stumbling for the next word. Her husband came to her aid.

"Father."

"Yes," she agreed. "My dear father."

"Well, it's the thought that counts, though, isn't it? Errare humanum est," Harold conceded.

"Oh," she asked. "Are you Spanish?"

"No," he answered.

"And not Jewish, either," Kuwak explained. "Mister Clump and I have already discussed that. He is an agnostic."

The doorbell rang. But before anyone could open it, the door opened and a handsome young man entered.

"Oh my God," Kuwak groaned, addressing the intruder. "Not you again. Don't you ever knock?"

"Now don't be rude, Dear," Mame admonished. "After all, Chip *is* our good friend, isn't he? And he *did* ring the doorbell after all. Didn't you, Chip dear?"

"Who's the gink?" Chip asked, apparently not too pleased with seeing Harold standing there.

"This is Mister Harold Clump," she said. "He's one of Dillon's new patients. He has a very interesting condition. He has an overly tight prepuce."

"A what?" Chip asked.

"His foreskin is too tight," Dr. Kuwak explained.

Everyone laughed except Harold.

"A funny thing about Mister Clump," Kuwak added, "is that he thought Fido was a real dog, and he brought the mutt in that basket in the corner there for Mame."

Everyone laughed heartily, again, except Harold.

Chip asked, "You mean that diamond and ruby doggy pin broach that I…ay, ay, ay,…that your father gave you as a family heirloom, Mame?"

"That's the one," Mame replied.

More uproarious laughter broke out between Mame and Chip.

"Ridere proprium humanitatis," Harold philosophically quoted Seneca.

He finally realized that what the two men at the club were talking about was a lost doggy pin, not a doggipin.

"Huh?" Chip said. "Is the gink Spanish?"

"No, Mame explained. "And he's not Jewish either. We've been all through that."

"It seems he's an agnostic," Kuwak added.

"Oh," Chip said, as though that explained everything.

"Dear," Mame addressed her husband. "It's Baby's feeding time. Go give him his bottle. *All* of it. Don't come back in here until Baby has finished every last drop."

"Again?" Kuwak whimpered.

"Again," Mame commanded. "After all, he is *your* baby."

Mame and Chip exchanged meaningful winks and smiles that did not go unnoticed by Harold.

"Oh, all right," the good doctor grumped. He shuffled off into the other room in none too happy a mood.

With the doctor out of the room, Chip said something to Harold that sounded rather rude. What he said was, "Okay Bud. That's the end of the party. Now take your goddam dog and beat it. Mame and I have some partying to do while the doc's out of the way. We need you out of the way, too, Pops."

Harold did not want to be present when the doctor returned from his feeding duties anyway. Nor did he want to be in the way of whatever the couple might have had in mind. He suspected it had to do with carnal knowledge.

He picked up the basket in the corner. Fido was still sleeping contentedly.

"Goodbye, you two," he said, and he was out the door.

Harold Clump took Fido back home to Dulzura and presented it to his wife as a present he had picked up in San Francisco just for her. She was pleased with his thoughtfulness.

Every evening from then on the Latin teacher has looked at the little doggy with great fondness. "Olim meminisse juvabit," he whispered in Fido's ears, assuring the doggipin that he would always be something to bring back sweet memories.

Or, at times, Harold quoted the sweet Bard of Avon in English.

When to the sessions of sweet silent thought
I summon up remembrance of things past…

ABOUT THE AUTHOR

Tim Desmondes was born and raised in Los Angeles. He has lived his entire life in California and has resided in many communities in that state.

Tim currently lives with his wife in a beach town in Southern California.

He is also the author of *Sex and Loathing In Hollywood*, a companion book to *Sexual Diversity and Perversity*, both published by Nazca Plains Corporation.